W9-CTS-173

"The sooner this is over, the better," she muttered under her breath, seeing no point in making herself heard.

His fingers were on the handle when she said it, but hear it he did—for in a flash he had turned, his jacket flailing out behind him like some outlaw provoked, and suddenly his face was level with her own and far, far too close.

She could feel his warm breath with startling awareness on her lips. It sent a prickle of excitement down her neck, across her skin and to the straining tips of her breasts. He reached out one finger to touch her jaw, the softness of the gesture mocking as he tilted her chin upward, his eyes dropping to her mouth.

"Oh, I will make it *better,* Tamara," he drawled, as if he could sense the sexual frustration teeming beneath her skin. "Better than anything you've ever experienced before. And it will be *soon.*"

SABRINA PHILIPS discovered the Harlequin® Presents line one Saturday afternoon in her early teens at her first job in a charity shop. Sorting through a stack of preloved books, she came across a cover featuring a glamorous heroine and a tall, dark, handsome hero. She started reading under the counter that instant and has never looked back!

A lover of both reading and writing, Sabrina went on to study English with classical studies at Reading University. She adores all literature but finds there's nothing else *quite* like enjoying the indulgent thrill of a Presents romance—preferably whilst lying in a hot bath with no distractions!

After graduating, Sabrina began to write in her spare time, but it wasn't until she attended a course run by Presents author Sharon Kendrick in a pink castle in Scotland that she realized if she wanted to be published badly enough, she had to *make* time. She wrote anywhere and everywhere and thankfully, it all paid off because a decade after reading her very first Harlequin® novel, her first submission, *Valenti's One-Month Mistress,* was accepted for publication in 2008. She is absolutely delighted to be an author herself and have the opportunity to create infuriatingly sexy heroes of her own, which she defies both her heroines—and her readers—to resist!

Sabrina continues to live in Guildford with her husband, who first swept her off her feet when they were both sixteen and poring over a copy of *Much Ado about Nothing* for their English A-Level. She loves traveling to exotic destinations and spending time with her family. When she isn't writing or doing one of the above, she works as deputy registrar of civil marriages, which she describes as a fantastic source of romantic inspiration and a great deal of fun.

For more information please visit
www.sabrinaphilips.com.

THE DESERT KING'S BEJEWELLED BRIDE

SABRINA PHILIPS

~ ROYAL AND RUTHLESS ~

TORONTO • NEW YORK • LONDON
AMSTERDAM • PARIS • SYDNEY • HAMBURG
STOCKHOLM • ATHENS • TOKYO • MILAN • MADRID
PRAGUE • WARSAW • BUDAPEST • AUCKLAND

If you purchased this book without a cover you should be aware
that this book is stolen property. It was reported as "unsold and
destroyed" to the publisher, and neither the author nor the
publisher has received any payment for this "stripped book."

Recycling programs
for this product may
not exist in your area.

ISBN-13: 978-0-373-52731-1

THE DESERT KING'S BEJEWELLED BRIDE

First North American Publication 2009.

Copyright © 2009 by Sabrina Philips.

All rights reserved. Except for use in any review, the reproduction or
utilization of this work in whole or in part in any form by any electronic,
mechanical or other means, now known or hereafter invented, including
xerography, photocopying and recording, or in any information storage
or retrieval system, is forbidden without the written permission of the
publisher, Harlequin Enterprises Limited, 225 Duncan Mill Road,
Don Mills, Ontario, Canada M3B 3K9.

This is a work of fiction. Names, characters, places and incidents are
either the product of the author's imagination or are used fictitiously,
and any resemblance to actual persons, living or dead, business
establishments, events or locales is entirely coincidental.

This edition published by arrangement with Harlequin Books S.A.

® and TM are trademarks of the publisher. Trademarks indicated with
® are registered in the United States Patent and Trademark Office, the
Canadian Trade Marks Office and in other countries.

www.eHarlequin.com

Printed in U.S.A.

THE DESERT KING'S
BEJEWELLED BRIDE

For Sharon Kendrick, to whom I owe so much.
And to Phil, for the perfect "I do."

CHAPTER ONE

'JUST lean *slightly* further forward—oh, *yes*, that's it.'

Kaliq clenched his teeth and resisted the urge to topple the balding excuse for a man who was leering behind the camera with such gusto that he was almost horizontal. The self-control it took not to step forward and silence him with a single flick of one long, lean finger required more resolve than he might have anticipated, for the scene was, after all, exactly as he had expected.

Unobserved in the shadows, Kaliq followed the man's lecherous gaze and bit down hard upon his lower lip as he slowly drank her in, the initial stab of recognition at seeing her again quite literally *in the flesh* mounting to a low insistent thud of desire in his groin. Hell, she was the very devil incarnate.

Splayed before a backdrop of fire, she was pouting provocatively, every inch of her offered up for his delectation—his, and every man's. Even if *technically* she wasn't naked, the shimmering slip of golden fabric—which back in Qwasir would be hard pushed to qualify as a mosquito net—barely skimmed her lush breasts before disappearing into nothing mid-thigh, and only served to enhance more of her slender figure than it covered. Never had he seen anything so close to, nor so far from his deepest fantasies both at the same time.

As the hot studio lights beat down upon her bronzed skin and those loose auburn curls, the irony forced him to suppress a sardonic laugh. Now, what was it she had said? That she wanted the freedom to live her life out of the spotlight that *his* attracted? Jezebel indeed, he thought, eyeing the logo on the oversized perfume bottle that was supposedly the central prop of the photo shoot but which one might be forgiven for overlooking completely.

It had been on his trip to the Qwasirian embassy in Paris last month that he had first caught a split-second glimpse of a billboard plastered with the inviting image of a woman all at once too familiar and yet not familiar enough. Then suddenly those deceptively wide eyes and rosebud lips had been everywhere, and even the swift investigation of his closest aide was unable to prove that he was mistaken. It *was* Tamara Weston. Never before had anything made him so furious.

He should have suspected as much. After all, even when she had been a guest in his land—not yet a woman and yet hardly a girl—she had been too spirited, both for her age and her sex, however prim she had looked. But seven years ago, accompanying her irrefutable allure had been an innocence he had foolishly believed was as much a part of her as her beauty. Kaliq's nostrils flared. What was it then, which had made her turn down the honour he had offered her in favour of *this*? Had the idea of sharing her body with only one man failed to excite her? Or was it her own limelight she had sought all along?

No matter, he thought, leaning back languorously against the doorframe. He might not be able to turn back the clock, take back the misplaced respect he had once bestowed upon her, but the future was a different story. This time, her *choice* didn't come into it. There was no question of his being mistaken about that.

* * *

As another lewd stage-direction passed Henry's lips, Tamara allowed her mind to wander. Just what expression would cross his oily features if she leaned far enough forward to swipe the smutty look off his face?

Ignore him, she told herself, unsure why she was letting him get to her today. *Every job has its downside*. Heavens, she should know. In the last few years she'd had more jobs than she could count on her fingers, and probably her toes as well. But take the odd walking slime-ball like Henry out of the equation—and thankfully his presence at these photo shoots was rare—and she had to admit that modelling had a lot more upsides than she would ever have imagined. *If* she had stopped to consider it as a potential career before now, which she hadn't. For, though she was tall at five foot nine and had inherited her mother's striking colouring and good bone structure, she would never have described her appearance as anything other than average. And after witnessing her parents' divorce splashed across the papers, she had never had the desire to forge any kind of career which would involve being in the public eye. However, when her college friend Lisa—who in Tamara's mind had that enviable fortune of knowing what she wanted to do with her life since the age of six—had asked her to pose wearing her first collection of fashion designs, she had agreed as a favour. To Tamara's amazement, when Lisa hit the big time, retail giant Jezebel Cosmetics had approached *her* with an offer to become the new face of their brand.

At first Tamara had been reluctant to accept, but when she saw the salary they were offering, she knew she couldn't pass up the opportunity to at least *try* a job which would allow her to give more than just her spare time to Mike. What she hadn't expected was to discover that there was much more to the job than simply looking sultry for a few hours a day; because aside from being mentally and physically exhausting, she had to work out the best way to convey whatever emotion the piece required. She found that satisfyingly challenging—even if, when she stopped to think about it, that might have been because portraying whatever image she was asked prevented her having to contemplate who *she* really was. As for the pace of it all; yes, she would gladly lose the press intrusion, but travelling to new destinations and meeting new people outweighed all of that. The point was, after flitting from one job to another, she actually felt as if she might be on the cusp of finding her place in the world, a sensation she hadn't had in years, not since…she had been in a very different place, a long time ago.

And, since becoming the new face of Jezebel Fragrance, fashion houses and magazine critics alike were hailing her the hottest new property in the modelling world. In the space of a few months she had gone from being just another girl in the sea of faces, to being recognised wherever she went, with photo shoots the world over. In fact, only yesterday Henry's assistant had informed her that next week she was expected in the Middle East and she couldn't wait.

But today, the moment she had walked out into the studio, she had felt ill at ease, as if there had been some kind of chemical reaction in the room and all the good had evaporated. Suddenly it seemed as if it was not just her appearance that was on display to the world, but her soul too. She couldn't put her finger on why. Henry's comments were no worse than usual. Her dress, the evocative backdrop was no different from countless other shoots. Was it perhaps down to the extra cameras that Henry's assistant had mentioned they would be using? She moved her legs beneath her uncomfortably, focusing on the multitude of people and equipment she usually pretended were not there at all. The forest of lenses and cables all angled towards her looked no denser than normal, and certainly no more alarming. Yet still the incongruous sense that she was being watched somehow *differently*, her instinct screaming at her to run, escape now before it was too late.

Telling herself she had just got out of the wrong side of bed that morning, she flicked her head to the left as instructed, allowing her mass of thick, dark hair to fall over her shoulder, and berated herself for her overactive imagination. However, the moment she did so, she caught sight of something on the periphery of her vision. Or, more specifically, some*one*. A tall figure shrouded in darkness, set apart from everyone else.

Tamara felt her heart stop beating and rise like the bubble in a thermometer, lodging itself in her throat. *Don't be stupid*, she told herself, unable to discern his face without altering her pose. It couldn't be. *He* would never be *here*. It was probably just another potential client of Henry's—a regular occurrence since Jezebel sales figures had gone through the roof. Yet, try as she might to rationalise the instinct which told her it was *not* just anyone, it was too overwhelming.

'Lov-ing that flushed look of expectancy, Tamara. Keep at that angle.'

But Tamara wasn't listening, for she had already turned her head. And, the instant she did, the air left her lungs as if someone had dealt a blow to her stomach.

Or her heart.

She would know that profile anywhere. The rugged, regal set of his features. The proud dark head. The autocratic posture of his tall, sculpted frame. That was what made her sure it was him. Other men might be as tall, their bodies just as athletically proportioned, but no one else stood like that. Head and shoulders above the rest, and not just literally. For he emanated an infuriatingly justified self-confidence. He knew that the moment he walked into a room, whether he was announced as Kaliq Al-Zahir A'zam, crown prince of Qwasir, or not, the particles in the air changed a little, so that every woman—no, every human being—was aware of the presence of a man who could not be ignored.

She swallowed and closed her eyes in disbelief, wishing that the heat spreading through her body would somehow make her invisible, camouflaged against the flames projected behind her. But she only felt herself growing more conspicuous, naked almost, beneath his dark, penetrating gaze.

Why on earth was he here? Had he some financial interest in Jezebel Cosmetics? It *was* one of the world's most successful new brands, but since when did a sheikh need to dabble in the retail industry for extra cash? He bought racehorses like other people bought popcorn, for goodness' sake—to liven up a little light entertainment. Tamara would have laughed at her own pathetic supposition if her heart wasn't pulsating so wildly, and if all her attention wasn't focused on looking anywhere but in his direction.

Why, then? Surely, after all this time, he hadn't come to remind her what she was missing, as if she was a task that had finally got to the top of his royal to-do list? No, he had made it perfectly clear that he *never* wanted to see her again. There had to be some logical explanation.

'All right, Tamara. Whilst the sight of your shivering side profile opens up a whole new realm of…possibilities, it rather detracts from the heat of the piece. Let's call it a day.'

For once, Tamara was actually grateful to hear Henry's voice. Plagued with curiosity though she was, the need to escape was greater. If she was quick, she could make a dash for her dressing room behind the main stage and leave by the back door. Because, no matter how unimaginable his reason for being here, never discovering it was preferable to facing her greatest regret head-on. It was bad enough that it had followed her around like a shadow all these years.

But quick, she soon discovered, had not been quick enough. For, as she slung on her jacket and hot-footed the short distance to her dressing room and flung open the door, it became apparent that he had been quicker.

'Kaliq!'

She did not know why she drew a breath in surprise. If his purpose was to speak with her, she knew he would not let a little matter like her reluctance interfere with his plans. With one leg tossed casually over the other, his suspended foot working impatiently, he sat back in the chair positioned right in the middle of her dressing room as if it were a throne. Waiting.

Tamara dared not meet his eyes: close up was fifty times more dangerous than taking in that lethal gaze from a distance. She had never seen him outside of Qwasir itself, and it struck her now more than it ever had before just how exotic he looked—that olive skin, the opulence of his thick, black hair which, while cut short, had a definite wave that seemed to speak of wildness and control at the same time. Although he wore his dark, impeccably cut suit as if he had been born into it, seeing him in Western dress seemed only to enhance just how much an extension of the untameable desert he was.

She remained at the doorway, fighting the contradicting emotions inside her which fought for supremacy. One half hating him—the only man she had ever believed herself in love with—for waltzing through the door just when she had finally started to forget, the other half feeling as if she had just woken up from a dull and lifeless sleep and discovered it was the first day of spring. The recollection that she ought to have bowed in the presence of the crown prince and that her informal address no doubt broke a thousand codes of Qwasirian conduct came later, and was the easiest to dismiss. Though perhaps not for him, for his eyes flicked over her with such censure that she felt if she didn't say something—anything—then the room would combust.

'Believe it or not, I wasn't expecting guests.' Tamara made a point of looking at the clothes and make-up scattered around the room, hoping it explained the look of horror on her treacherously expressive face.

'Don't tell me that acting is another of your hidden talents,' he drawled, eyeing the bouquet on her dressing table, which she had hastily plonked in water before the start of the shoot. 'It can hardly be an unusual occurrence to find an admirer hovering in your dressing room, hmm?'

Tamara felt herself colour involuntarily at the insinuation, all the more so because blushing was a childhood tendency that until now she had thought she'd grown out of. The flowers were just a thank you from Mike, but she might have guessed that, to Kaliq, modelling and a lack of virtue were synonymous. Did he suppose she had a different admirer in here every day of the week? How little he knew.

'Actually, it is—'

'There is no need to play the innocent with me *now*, Tamara,' he interjected.

'Didn't anyone ever teach you to allow a person to finish their sentence?'

Kaliq suddenly raised his head, as if the concept of someone correcting him was entirely alien and he needed to check he had heard correctly.

'I was about to say that most people pay attention to the *private* sign on the door.' The words rebounded in her head as soon as she had spoken them. Kaliq was many things, but he most certainly was not *most people*.

'Privacy is not a luxury I'm well acquainted with.' His eyes narrowed. 'Occupational hazard, as someone once pointed out to me.'

Tamara cringed as she recognised the words she had once spoken, even as a small, foolish part of her leaped that he remembered. Until she realised that in ignoring the sign he'd just proved that he still didn't give a damn about anyone's wishes but his own.

She stiffened. 'And yet you were always so strict on matters of propriety, I seem to recall.'

'Just as I recall you saying that you could never bear a life in the public eye. And yet now you are recognised the world over. It is funny, is it not, how things change?' Kaliq feigned a puzzled look. 'Or perhaps I was mistaken?'

He was *never* mistaken, and she knew it. He leaned back with amusement and awaited her response. Much as sitting here, hearing her *try* to defend herself made him want to crush the arms of the chair beneath his hands, he was enjoying himself.

He still got to her. He could see it in the flush of colour that had begun somewhere above the rounds of her breasts. It had risen between the 'V' created by her hastily slung on jacket and up that long, slender neck of hers, which reminded him of a bird at an oasis. And it had stained her cheeks almost from the moment she had walked in and found him here. When she had been trying to escape.

She would not escape. That much was certain. No matter how much she protested her innocence or faked a blush. He would show no restraint. For the boundary he had once forbidden himself to cross had now undoubtedly been torn. Yet, though he knew her virtue was lost, just looking at her sent flames of desire licking through his body. Even more surprisingly, he was overpowered by a greater need. To do this slowly. It was understandable, he supposed. He should have had her then. Though he had waited long enough, where would be the sense in not savouring the moment? Like an eagle who had spent a long night parched in the desert, why swoop in on the first sight of the perfect kill without care and precision? Better to hold back and wait for the slow, defined culmination of all that had gone before.

'Just tell me why you're here, Kaliq.' Tamara hugged her soft brown jacket around her and buttoned it up to the neck as if the gesture might encourage him to leave. If he registered the less than subtle hint, the unwavering set of his jaw told her its impact had been about as effective as a pellet gun shot into bullet-proof glass.

Surely he hadn't come all this way to simply throw her words back at her? Yes, she *had* told him she could never have dealt with the fame his royal status attracted, but she would have said anything that held an element of truth rather than let him know just how deeply he had hurt her. As she recalled it, he had barely listened anyway. She knew that whatever reason she had given didn't matter, only that his expression had turned to pure hatred the minute she had shaken her head. So why would it matter now?

'Patience is a virtue, Tamara. Surely even you are still capable of that one?'

Tamara felt her blood boil in anger. 'Better to lose virtues than to gain defects, Your Highness.' She dropped into a mocking bow. 'You used to at least *pretend* to respect all people in equal measure. Now I see that only goes for people who obey your every whim.'

Kaliq's eyes glittered up at her. 'Then it is lucky you have a chance to make good on your transgression.'

Tamara felt every muscle in her body tense. Surely he hadn't come to ask her…surely he didn't think—did he?

He paused with all the superiority of a man who was used to people hanging on his every word. 'I have come to hire you.'

'*Hire* me?' He made her sound like a power tool he needed for some tricky palace DIY.

'Do not sound so surprised, Tamara. This is what you do, is it not? Appear however and wherever you are paid to do so.'

His words made her ashamed of the first thing she had felt proud of in years.

He continued, oblivious. 'Which answers your question as to why I am here.'

'What are you talking about?'

'I want you to model for me.'

'Model what?'

'The A'zam Sapphires.'

CHAPTER TWO

THE A'zam Sapphires?

Tamara stared in disbelief at his inscrutable expression, telling herself to keep breathing in and out.

To anyone else it might sound as if she had just been offered the biggest scoop of her whirlwind career—the honour of being asked to model the royal jewels of Qwasir, the most ancient and precious sapphires on earth—but Tamara knew that honour had nothing to do with it. This was about revenge. Because they weren't just valuable heirlooms, or stones so remarkably blue they had their own shade of Dulux paint named after them— they were the gems traditionally worn when the crown prince took a bride. The jewels she might have worn. For real.

Yes, he knew all about offering what *looked* like perfection on a plate, but there was no way she was going to agree to play his glorified mannequin. Tamara opened her mouth to tell him as much, but the instant she did the door burst open behind her.

'Your Highness, Prince A'zam, my sincere apologies—I had no idea you had arrived!' Henry entered in a whirlwind of half-bowed haste. 'My assistant has only just informed me—oh, you simply can't get the staff—I would have sent a car immediately if I had known, forgive me. Please, allow me to get you a drink—'

Tamara shut her mouth again, disquiet rippling through her. Henry had been *expecting* him? Was he somehow in on this whole preposterous scheme?

Kaliq raised his hand and motioned for Henry to stand up straight. Tamara wished he hadn't bothered. If he had gone much longer without taking a breath he might have exploded in a frenzy of over-exaggerated gesticulation, and so much the better if he had taken Kaliq with him.

'No matter,' Kaliq ground out, his eyes blazing as they trailed Henry's unannounced path through the door and into her dressing room. 'As you can see, Miss Weston afforded me the same pleasurable intimacy it seems she grants everyone.'

He turned to her, a damning expression playing across his outrageously sensual mouth. 'You really must take down that "private" sign and replace it with something more appropriate. *Unrestricted access*, perhaps?'

Henry grinned, showing two rows of yellowing teeth. 'Oh, yes, Tamara's a blessing to work with, not another ice-queen like most models these days, if you know what I mean.' Henry winked at Kaliq as if they were in some sort of private men's club and nodded to Tamara as if he had paid her a priceless compliment.

'I know exactly what you mean,' Kaliq replied, his words deliberate, sending an ominous chill from the nape of Tamara's neck down to her tailbone. 'In fact, I believe Tamara was just about to express her *enthusiasm* for the news that her next assignment will be working for me.' He looked at her expectantly, but Henry cut in.

'And who can blame her? The Jezebel girl modelling royal jewels—how's that for publicity?' He grinned smarmily all over his face and for the second time that day, and more vehemently than before, Tamara was overcome with the urge to slap him. So Kaliq *had* gone through Henry to get to her. This wasn't—oh, God, *this* was the shoot in the Middle East that Emma had mentioned in passing and that she had been looking forward to?

'Actually—' her voice came out louder than she intended and suddenly both men's eyes were upon her, one greedily, the other indifferently, as if this was a done deal '—what I was about to say is that—*honoured* though I am that you thought of me, *Your Highness*, I have no wish to accept your offer.'

If the scene had been drawn in a comic book, by the time Tamara's sarcastic words had hit the air, steam would have been billowing from Henry's ever-reddening ears. Oblivious to the atmosphere in the room that spoke of a past of which he knew nothing, he turned on Tamara as if she were a petulant child throwing a tantrum for no reason other than to irritate him.

'You are contracted to Jezebel Limited and, since His Royal Highness has *wisely* organised this unique modelling opportunity through the company, I'm afraid your impetuous wants, or in this case *won'ts*, count for nothing.'

Henry guffawed as if he had made the joke of the year, and looked at Kaliq for approval, which didn't come.

'Everyone has a choice,' she said, her voice low, looking directly at Kaliq. 'Just because someone expects you to perform a certain duty does not mean you have to fall in line.'

For the first time she saw something like emotion flicker in Kaliq's eyes. *Good*, she thought to herself, even if it was nothing more than wounded pride.

Henry moved bullishly towards her. 'You turn this down and you kiss your contract with Jezebel goodbye, Tamara.'

Kaliq abruptly stood up between them, the sheer size of him forcing Henry to take a step back.

'Thank you—Henry, is it? I am sure Miss Weston is just a little daunted by the enormity of the task. She is bound to be nervous about the proper behaviour—*so* unfamiliar to her—that will be required in Qwasir. Please leave us, I will put her mind at rest.'

Consumed with frustration that in one fell swoop Kaliq had branded her devoid of both integrity and the ability to stand up for herself, Tamara watched Henry reluctantly depart. She didn't bother to listen for the sound of his footsteps walking away, for he viewed every chance of a bigger bonus for himself with even hungrier eyes than he ogled every woman who moved. She knew he would not let her determine one of the most lucrative and high profile deals of his career without eavesdropping, regardless of Kaliq's dismissal. But she didn't care. This was not about Henry.

This was about Kaliq, as far too many things in her life had already been. Turning her body back round purposefully, she came up against his with a start. In the split second she had turned away, he had silently homed in upon her like some deadly heat-seeking missile. For all the cover it offered her, she wished she had not primly fastened her jacket, her body now flooding with warmth as the distinctive, spicy scent of him filled her nostrils. Sandalwood. Amber. She shook herself. No, she would not forget her resolve just because his sex appeal was so damned potent.

'You might have grown used to your position and your wealth ensuring that you have everything you desire, Kaliq, but, I promise you, you will not have me.'

She hadn't meant it to come out like that. She took a step back, her cheeks growing an even brighter shade of crimson. There was no question of him wanting her. Even then she had been nothing to him but a row of ticks on a checklist of suitable attributes.

'Come, Tamara, do not pretend that finding yourself in this position is not precisely what you truly desire.' His eyes blazed with contempt. 'The display of the royal jewels shall be televised worldwide. There will be dignitaries, royalty, the world's social elite. Exactly the exposure you crave. There is no need to feign shyness.'

'I signed a contract to Henry, not to you.'

His jaw tensed. 'Yes. With your abandonment of morality also went shrewd judgement, it seems.'

'And yet you are in cahoots with him yourself, to use me in any way that suits you. Are the two of you so different, I wonder?'

He did not rise to the bait. 'What do you think?' He looked at her with arrogant self-assurance. 'I will pay what he pays you in a year for this one job. Turn me down and you lose both.'

Tamara knew that Kaliq's fortune totalled more figures than would fit on the screen of most calculators, but she also knew that he didn't make excessive offers just for the sake of it. He wanted this badly, and he had planned it like a chess player manoeuvring pieces on a board involving Henry to trap her. But the truth was that Henry and Kaliq were no more alike than a sewer rat and a mountain lion, and part of her, though she loathed the thought of the blackmail he proposed, wanted to look into his eyes and say yes. Because she and Mike could do so much good with that money. Because, if she took her personal feelings out of it, professionally, it was an incredible opportunity. And mostly because, even though it went against every word she had repeated like a mantra since walking away from this man, she had felt more alive these last ten minutes than she had done in years.

Tamara tore her eyes away from him and began to busy her hands tidying some of the clothes on the chair beside her.

Looking at him was too dangerous. His smooth skin was as tempting as her favorite decadent chocolate dessert, his long lean hands reminded her of how he had once held her before him with so much tenderness and power. What would coming back from the dizzying heights of being a part of his world for a second time in her life do to her when he was so blatantly setting out to wound her?

'You already have my answer. I am sure you will have no trouble finding someone else.'

'I do not want anyone else.'

Tamara almost dropped the skirt she was folding and had to blink to stop her imagination running away with her, but he continued.

'My father is unwell.' His voice was uncharacteristically strained as he began to pace the floor. 'The world's press is full of the King's impending demise, and the people of my country are ill at ease. I wish to distract them from his deteriorating health by showcasing Qwasir's oldest and most precious treasure at a royal gala.' She watched his face, like a poker player about to reveal his ace, and the cynicism in his tone returned. 'Who better for the task than the model whose name is on everyone's lips, who also happens to be the daughter of a former Qwasirian ambassador? The headlines will write themselves.'

Fighting against a pang of empathy which she could not give room to, Tamara drew in a ragged breath, heavy with new understanding. So that was it. She had read about King Rashid's poor health and she understood just why his people would be unsettled, understood much more than she wished. Because the crown prince *had* to marry in order to inherit. Parading the jewels would convince them that he planned to take a bride, and soon.

So she *was* to be used as a pawn. How foolish to think he had enough of a heart for this to be personal. He wanted her as nothing more than a political diversion, like a magician's assistant used to captivate his audience's attention. She watched as he wandered over to the window, looking out at the busy London traffic. For an instant it surprised her that the outside world was still turning. It felt as if nothing existed outside this room, but this wasn't about them—it was just a tactical manoeuvre. For some reason, acknowledging that seemed to allow her to push her emotions aside. This really was business, so why should she toss away her modelling contract because of him? Wouldn't that be surrendering the freedom to live her life however she chose, when that was the one thing she had always fought for? Much worse, wouldn't refusing make him think that a part of her, however small, re-gretted the past?

No, she wouldn't let that happen. It was just a business trip like any other, and afterwards, aside from keeping her job, maybe she would finally be able to lay the shadow of the past behind her, to stop wondering if she'd made the right decision and *know* she had. For hadn't the last fifteen minutes gone some way to proving it?

'Model the jewels for one evening, for the sum of my annual Jezebel contract?' she repeated, her tone as matter-of-fact as she could muster.

Kaliq turned from the window, his mouth a thin, hard line. So, contrary to whatever she had made him believe back then, she *was* no different. She could be manipulated by the promise of money and fame as easily as every other woman he knew. It just hadn't been quite tempting enough to tie herself to only one man. But then she hadn't been tied to *him* yet, had she?

'Five days from today.'

For a minute she looked at him as if he was mad, convinced that not even he was capable of organising an event of such scope in less than a week, but then she realised. It was already all arranged, wasn't it? He was just waiting for her to slot into place. Again. That annoyed her more than everything else about this whole set-up put together.

'What if I refuse? You'll just cancel the whole thing?'

He gave her a withering smile. 'If *I* was not present, there would be no event. If *you* decide you would rather throw away your *career* than do a few hours' work, I can assure you I will have no trouble finding a willing replacement.'

She looked at him stonily. Knowing he was right. Hating him for it.

He continued as if her agreement had never been in question. 'Naturally, in the interim you will be required for a few other tasks—' he ran his eyes over her in blatant sensual appraisal '—rehearsals for the event, et cetera. Aside from that, you may spend your time however you wish.'

Wishing myself anywhere else, no doubt, she thought, wondering what choice she had and attempting to loosen her shoulders. But she failed; every muscle in her body was too taut from the sheer thrill of being near him. No, five days in his company might not cure *that*, but at least now she was old enough now not to mistake his favourable blend of genes for something else entirely.

'I will collect you from your apartment tomorrow, at eleven.'

Kaliq flexed his broad shoulders and moved towards the door. Tamara was not sure why she was surprised that he already knew where she lived, let alone why she had supposed he might stick around, if only to gloat. Of course not. To talk, to chat over dinner, perhaps, was far beyond the realms of what a future king would bestow upon *her*, for she was not to be treated as anything other than a portable window display. No, he was too cold, too ruthlessly efficient for that. Her submission today was just another detail he had executed with the same cool rationality he had used to discover where she was. Evidently she had already taken up too much of his precious time.

'The sooner this is over, the better,' she muttered under her breath, seeing no point in making herself heard.

His fingers were on the handle when she said it, but hear it he did. In a flash he had turned, his jacket flaring out behind him like some outlaw provoked, and suddenly his face was level with her own and far, far too close.

She could feel his warm breath with startling awareness on her lips. It sent a prickle of excitement down her neck, across her skin and to the straining tips of her breasts. He reached out one finger to touch her jaw, the softness of the gesture mocking as he tilted her chin upwards, his eyes dropping to her mouth.

'Oh, I will make it *better*, Tamara,' he drawled, as if he could sense the sexual frustration teeming beneath her skin. 'Better than anything you've ever experienced before, and it will be *soon*.'

He moved his head a fraction closer, too close to think about anything but kissing him. Tamara closed her eyes and leaned in instinctively. But in one swift movement he dropped his finger from her chin and reached for her hand with his and, tantalisingly slowly, he raised it to his mouth.

Somehow, the gesture—masquerading as modest etiquette—felt so intimate that it had her legs almost buckling beneath her. The feel of his lips on her bare skin was far hotter than the studio lights had been, igniting a desire within her so unchecked it left her scared of what she might do next. He looked at her from beneath hooded lids with such intensity that she had to remind herself to breathe. She tore her gaze away from him.

'Kaliq, this is business, nothing more.' Her voice was husky, breathless.

He didn't answer, but released the hand he had kissed, before running his fingers up her arm and resting his hand in her hair, his thumb reaching out to gently stroke her bottom lip. It took all the willpower she had not to taste it with the tip of her tongue. As he watched her eyes widen he raised the corner of his mouth in a wry smile.

'I'm glad we agree. *Unfinished* business. But not for much longer.'

With that, he broke away from her and flung open the door, Henry scuttling in his wake and Tamara reeling.

CHAPTER THREE

IT WAS the kiss that did it. The kiss that she couldn't drive from her mind. And for goodness' sake it had only been his lips pressed to her hand! What the hell would she have been like if he had kissed any other part of her body?

Don't even go there, she warned herself as she tossed aside the covers, through with trying to sleep. For even when tiredness had finally overtaken her, she had woken hot and breathless with images of her body pressed to his—for some pathetic reason wearing nothing but the damned sapphires—blazing through her mind.

Tamara sat up against the headboard, taking the weight of her hair in her hands and allowing the cool air to reach the damp nape of her neck as she stared into the darkness, feeling ashamed. She knew that what had passed between them had nothing to do with any genuine desire on his part; he had simply been using his natural ability to play to women's fantasies to get what he wanted and it had worked. Until he had touched her she had at least felt marginally in control, but the split second that he raised her hand to his lips she was transported back seven years as if she had fallen through some gap in space and time, all self-protection stripped from her in the process.

But then actions spoke louder than words, didn't they say?

They were like a familiar scent that could recall another time and place in an instant. The minute he had touched her that way she was no longer the twenty-six-year-old model standing in her dressing room with her jacket buttoned fast around her, forced to make a choice that was doomed either way. No, when he'd raised her hand to his lips she was that wide-eyed teenager again, the world at her feet.

The girl she had been the summer she'd turned nineteen, when it had seemed her life was truly about to begin, she thought wretchedly. Because, although on paper it had always looked to be a life full of potential—the daughter of a West End actress and a great foreign diplomat, the reality had been nothing so sensational. Her father's work abroad and her mother's gruelling schedule had led them to divorce when she was still at junior school and, by the age of thirteen, boarding school had become the place she grudgingly called home. Though her father would send gifts galore from the places he'd visited, and her dorm was stacked full of her mother's memorabilia, she would gladly have swapped them all for the odd family holiday or the chance to have done something more notable than sit her A levels and watch the Wimbledon finals with her school friends. And whilst they'd been happy choosing college courses and eyeing up the boys from the local school, Tamara had been restless, dreaming of finding her own place in the world. She certainly had no desire to remain in the classroom, or to repeat her parents' failed attempt at love.

So when her father had announced that he wished her to visit him in the Middle East for a week, it had felt as if the door to her future had at last been flung open. As if finally she was on the cusp of…something. And Qwasir! She remembered rolling the word over in her mouth like an exotic delicacy for weeks before her ticket had even arrived, immersing herself in every book she could find on the country, noting down snippets of information as if they were bright keys to her future.

When the plane had finally touched down, she was not disappointed. Qwasir had not only met, but surpassed her wildest imaginings. From the minute she'd been met by the black royal-crested Jeep at the airport and driven through the town and out across the expansive desert landscape towards the royal palace, everything seemed full of so much colour, heat, life. As if all this time she'd been living in a rock pool and she had finally escaped into the wide, wide ocean.

Never more so than at the moment when the driver of the Jeep had led her through the enormous palace gates and asked Tamara to wait in the bright white marble atrium. It was such a maze of rooms and corridors that it put in her mind of the story of Theseus and the Minotaur, just asking to be explored.

Finding herself alone, Tamara had tiptoed towards the first doorway to the left, her eyes widening to discover a room full of glass display cases. It seemed to be a section of the palace open to public view. She wandered in, her eyes drawn to an original colour photograph of King Rashid and his late wife Sofia on their wedding day, an enlarged version of the black and white one she had so loved in her guidebook. Not because she had a penchant for all things bridal, but because of the look on Sofia's face, as if in that instant she had discovered where *she* truly belonged. It was then that Tamara's eyes had dropped to the glass case beneath the photo and widened in awe, for it contained the very necklace Sofia had worn in the picture, and which had been given more page-space in her guidebook than anything else—the famous A'zam Sapphires.

'I'm afraid we're closed for today.'

Tamara jumped at the discovery that she was not alone and swung round instantly to try to locate the origin of the deep voice that had seemed to come out of nowhere.

Leaning nonchalantly at the doorway was a man unlike any other she had seen before—and not just because of his Eastern dress. A man who stood as if not only she, but the whole world had turned to him. Who took her breath away and replaced it with heat and excitement.

'I'm sorry it's just—' she turned back to the case guiltily '—it's so beautiful I couldn't help but look.'

His dark eyes narrowed. 'They tend to have that effect—people not being able to help themselves. Which is why we only ever display a replica.'

Tamara looked puzzled for a moment. 'Actually, I was talking about the photograph.' His eyes widened, as if she had surprised him. 'It's a fascinating display. It must be a pleasure to work here.'

A look of amusement crossed his lips and she saw his expression visibly soften. '*Indeed*. And no doubt there will be time for you to continue your appraisal tomorrow, Miss Weston. In the meantime, let me show you where you will be staying.' He inclined his head towards the door. 'Your father sends his apologies that he is not here to meet you in person. He is still in a conference—on Qwasirian security.' He raised his eyebrow ironically.

'Tamara, please,' she offered. 'And, as it seems you already know, I am the daughter of James Weston. It's a pleasure to meet you…?' Tamara raised her eyebrows inquisitively.

'We have a tradition in Qwasir that guests and hosts share nothing but names until they have shared food together,' he offered in explanation, gesturing for her to follow him, though the slight curl of a smile at the corner of his mouth belied the severity of his tone.

'I had read that was so,' Tamara said equally levelly, though mischief was dancing in her eyes, 'but since you had already broken that tradition by surmising so much about me, I thought perhaps you were hoping I was unaware of the custom.'

He whipped his head round in shock and Tamara instantly wondered whether her quick-wittedness had offended him. But, as she raised her head anxiously, his eyes glittered back in amused challenge.

'Very well,' he said, facing her head-on and extending his hand to her, 'I am Kaliq Al-Zahir A'zam, and my father is King Rashid of Qwasir. Welcome to our palace.'

The crown prince!

Tamara felt instantly that she should drop into a reverent curtsy, but she was too overwhelmed and embarrassed to move. Of course he was royalty! Who else would be capable of giving off that aura of magnificence unlike any she had ever felt before? Though she knew that her father resided in a wing of the palace, she hadn't anticipated that she would come into contact with the A'zam family herself. According to the books she had read, the crown prince spent most of his time studying abroad. She didn't think he'd just be meandering round the palace where he might be mistaken for—oh, God, had she really supposed he was a museum steward?

Tamara blushed and extended her hand quickly in return, and was almost as shocked by the bolt of electricity his touch sent through her body as by the revelation of who he was. She bowed her head. 'It is an honour to meet you.'

To her surprise, she thought she heard him exhale wearily, but though it took every effort, she dared not look up.

But, to her astonishment, he lowered *his* head until her light blue eyes met the rich darkness of his. 'Kaliq, please.'

His gaze was too enthralling to hold. She turned away. 'I am sorry. I didn't expect… I didn't know what to expect.'

'You are not quite what I was expecting either.'

Tamara's eyes moved down over her pink and white gingham dress, her heart sinking. No doubt he must be used to women dropping at his feet immediately, either covered reverently in swathes of beautiful fabric, or buffered to such perfection that they resembled a female form of himself. She failed on both accounts.

'You misunderstand me, Tamara,' he said, slowing raising her hand to his lips, her eyes growing wider and her heart beating faster the closer he got. 'I find it very rare that I am surprised by anything of late. I had forgotten what a pleasure it is.'

It was then—as his lips touched her flesh—that Tamara suddenly raised her head and something passed between them. Something indescribable. That felt as old and unique as the treasures in that room, yet new and so much more precious.

For in that one statement and the glance that had followed, her feelings of unworthiness, her fear at having the wrong words, the wrong clothes, of being a world away from him, disappeared on the spot. As he gazed back at her she realised that underneath all that she was just a woman and he was just a man who might long to be something other than he was as much as she did, no matter how much colour his world held to her.

Had held to her *then*, Tamara corrected inwardly as she flicked on her bedside lamp. Not any more. Because, whatever she had once thought, she couldn't have got it more wrong. And the incredible week that had followed—the hours they had spent talking about anything and everything whilst her father was working, the life-changing day when he had taken her to the new school he'd had built and made her see how misguided she had been to think of her years of education as restrictive, hearing about his studies in Europe with his best friend Leon, encouraging her hopes to do the same—none of it had been about open-mindedness or respect at all. He had made her believe that the world was her oyster, and then tried to confine her to another rock pool, just different from the one she'd started in.

She would do well to try and remember that. Yesterday in her dressing room she ought to have known better than to allow herself to *feel* anything, she thought bleakly as she watched a tiny moth flit into the bulb of her bedside lamp again and again. At the very least she ought to have been capable of masking her emotions, as she did every day in front of the camera, even if she couldn't help surrendering to them at night.

Tamara picked up her mobile phone to check the time. Six-twenty a.m. One new message. She drew in a deep breath, her nerves on edge, but it was from Emma, Henry's assistant. She told herself to feel relieved.

Henry says PLEASE be on time for Prince A'zam. Good Luck. Emma xxx

As she read the words, she imagined herself waiting obediently in her hallway at eleven o'clock. The thought made her grimace. Surely there was another way to see this through. A way which didn't make her feel as if she'd already lost…

It was not, Tamara discovered, particularly easy to book a last minute flight, nor accommodation in the middle of the desert at half past six on a Tuesday morning, but the challenge at least gave her the satisfaction of doing *something* rather than just sitting there, passively awaiting her fate. She felt relieved knowing that this way she could see the job through and hang on to her independence without the distraction of Kaliq's formidable presence every time she turned around.

With the sun still low in the sky, she wheeled her suitcase down the steps from her flat. The flat she was still renting, even though she had saved enough for a deposit. Her landlord was happy to sell it to her, but she still couldn't bring herself to commit, even though it had plenty of good points. Like the fact it was just a short walk to the train station, which thankfully linked directly with the airport.

But just as she turned out of the gate to begin that familiar route, she caught sight of a low-slung vehicle with tinted windows on the opposite side of the street. Despite its understated metallic black bodywork, it looked as conspicuous as a panther in the Arctic. It was large and sleek, and she knew it was not the kind of car her neighbours could even afford to hire, let alone own. *Please*, she prayed to herself, let Penny downstairs have finally bagged her rich boss who she was always harping on about.

'Raring to go, Tamara?' The silky drawl that cut through the stillness of the morning as she reached the bottom of the steps made her jump, but the surge of adrenaline immediately turned to anger.

'Is stalking another pursuit you consider a royal right, along with blackmail, Kaliq?' she bit out, not bothering to stop walking.

'Just keeping an eye on what's mine.'

'I beg your pardon?' She stopped then, but didn't turn around, trying to ignore the way the endless expanse of cool morning air seemed to have grown claustrophobic with the throb of sexual awareness.

'You are my employee now, are you not? Since you have a tendency for not knowing what's good for you, I thought I'd make sure you didn't do anything stupid. It seems it was a precaution worth taking.'

'Then you're mistaken. I never go back on my word. Nor do I consider leaving early for an assignment to be stupid, do you?'

'My mistake indeed,' he whispered slowly as he came up behind her. 'I should have guessed that you were dying to start peeling off your clothes.'

'You didn't mention that I would be required to remove any clothes. I would appreciate it if you could clarify what is required of me, if my duties are not to be as I was initially informed.'

'I think you know perfectly well what is required of you.'

She swung round then. The slanted smile on his face read that he was keeping score and it was one-nil to him.

'I agreed to model some old jewels. Assuming that is what you mean, I think we understand each other.'

She saw a nerve work at his jaw and visualised a score board depicting one-all.

'You make it sound as if what I ask you to do makes a difference to your answer, Tamara. I hardly think you need to pretend your standards are so exacting.'

God, he really was from the Dark Ages! It wasn't as if she posed for page three, for goodness' sake—she'd never been photographed in anything less than what most people wore to the supermarket in summer, and usually a lot more. But then he was *trying* to get her, wasn't he?

'I wasn't pretending any such thing,' she answered coolly. 'What you ask of me simply makes a difference to how much I charge.'

'And how much do you charge, Tamara, for say—one night?'

Tamara glowered at him. 'Sex may be written into the

contract of every other one of your female employees, Kaliq, but it is not in mine.'

'What makes you think it needs to be written in,' he purred, 'when you know it goes without saying?'

Tamara felt a wave of heat rush over her, which threatened to drag her mind back to the place it had been in the early hours of the morning, but she tore herself away from his mesmerising look of intent, turned on her heel and began to walk down the street.

'Where the hell do you think you're going?'

'To catch my train.'

'Then clearly, Tamara, you are not charging enough.' Kaliq reached out and caught hold of her arm, spinning her round to face him.

'Public transport may be an alien concept to you, *Your Highness*—' Tamara shook out of his grip as she motioned towards the costly vehicle on the opposite side of the street '—but I can assure you it is a perfectly adequate means of travel.'

'But why have adequate, Tamara, when you can have the best?' He drawled, 'My private jet is waiting.'

'As is my charter flight and city accommodation.'

Kaliq looked utterly exasperated. 'You think it is safe for a young woman to travel and stay alone in Qwasir?'

'If it wasn't, I would imagine the crown prince would have bigger concerns than hanging around here just to make sure he had someone to wear a necklace four days from now.'

Kaliq's eyes darkened. 'It is a fact of life that our cultures are different, Tamara.'

Tamara nodded and reached for the handle of her case once more. 'You would do well to remember it. See you there.'

'I'm afraid not, Tamara.'

'What the hell does that mean?'

'It means I require you in one piece for what I have in mind. Travelling in my transport and staying in my palace have just been added to the list of what is required of you. Now, get in the car.'

CHAPTER FOUR

As TAMARA sank back into the obscenely comfortable seat and looked out at the mushroom-like clouds below, she told herself she was glad. After all, having to put up with his pre-historic demands for the duration of this assignment was one of the reasons why she'd agreed to it. For what could be more cathartic than to return home a week from now, knowing for certain that she could *never* have endured him?

She ought to be glad that he was making it so easy for her—that he was giving her every opportunity to harden her heart, to adopt the ice-cool, businesslike demeanour that Henry had described as customary in every other model he knew. Yet nothing about this felt easy.

Maybe it was because she hadn't expected him to act in that cool manner himself. From the minute they had set foot on his private jet, he had positioned himself at the opposite end of the flight deck and immersed himself in a briefcase full of paperwork as if she were nothing more than a piece of excess baggage which didn't fit in the hold. The few times he had looked up he had glanced straight through her, as if she had ceased to exist.

But then that was how he worked, wasn't it? Oh, yes, her every mile-high whim would be catered for by his staff, but the minute she fell in line with his plans she ceased to matter to him. Because *nothing* mattered to him except his precious crown, she thought wretchedly. Until now she had been in danger of forgetting that.

Of forgetting that night.

Tamara squinted out at the view, the clouds becoming less dense and the yellow-brown hue of the desert landscape below just starting to become visible. The sight made her ball up the thin jumper she had been wearing and place it between her head and the window, pretending she wanted to sleep. The reality was she simply wanted to block out the view. To block out the memories.

It had been at the end of her stay in Qwasir—though leaving was something she had not allowed herself to contemplate— when the two of them and his aide had ridden across that desert at dusk. Kaliq had been insistent that she experience the annual masked festival in the tiny mountain village near the royal palace. She suspected she would have nodded in wide-eyed awe at whatever he'd suggested, but knowing that for one night no one would be able to recognise him as the crown prince had particularly delighted her. Perhaps because she'd grown tired of dodging the press whenever she was with him—ten times worse than the intrusion she had experienced on the few occasions a year she spent time with her mother. Perhaps because *she'd* wanted to forget exactly who he was.

For in Tamara's eyes, his title had seemed detached from him, like a middle name rarely used. To her, he was the man who'd taught by example to defy what was expected, who'd made her recognise that she had been short-sighted, ungrateful even, to have been disappointed with her experiences in life so far, and who had encouraged her to pursue *her* dreams the way no one else ever had. Almost more startling, he'd made her want to venture into territory that—unlike everyone else her age—she had never wanted to sample before. She'd wanted him physically. To explore him—have him explore her. And, though he'd insisted it was necessary that they travel with an aide, the smouldering look in his eyes had seemed to say that the feeling was mutual.

So when, after a night of drinking the dark, spicy local drink and dancing anonymously amongst the jovial crowds, they'd left in the early hours of the morning with his aide nowhere in sight, Tamara's heart thrilled at the thought of being alone with him. Had he engineered it on purpose? She'd felt sure that he had. Though she didn't know what that meant in the long-term, it didn't seem to matter. Because, for the first time in her life, instead of wondering where she might be going, she could think only of the here and now. Of her body pressed to his back, the sounds of the festival dying away and their breathing perfectly in time as they'd ridden over the hilltop to the incredible sight of the sun rising over the sand dunes. It had felt as if the thermostat which had been keeping her feelings at bay had just gone up in flames.

'Please, Kaliq, let's stop for a moment, it's so perfect.'

Kaliq didn't answer, but suddenly through the half-light she saw that they were making their way downwards to a small gap in the mountainside, his horse Amir now slowing to a walk.

Hesitantly, Kaliq dismounted and raised his arms to lift her from his stallion. He looked, she thought, rather as if he were considering waging war against himself.

He moved away from her, looking out towards the rising sun. 'We should really get back to the palace. It is late.'

'Or perhaps we are just up early; it depends how you look at it.'

'You should be asleep.' His face was solemn.

Tamara frowned. Usually he delighted in the habit she had of turning everything he said on its head. She followed his serious gaze, to the tip of gold shimmering on the horizon, and then back to his face. 'You think I would rather be asleep than here, with you?'

'No, Tamara.' He shook his head, his expression taut. 'I think your father trusted me to show you my country. He did not ask that I find myself alone in the desert with you in the early hours of morning. It is not *right*.'

Right? Nothing had ever felt more right in her entire life. What was he saying—that she was nothing more to him than a puppy he had been given to walk, but this was past his agreed hours?

'I am not a child, Kaliq. In a month I may be travelling through Europe, next year university, who knows? Do you suppose I will never *find myself alone* with anyone then?'

A muscle tensed at his jaw.

Tamara continued. 'If I am taking up too much of your precious time then I will quite gladly continue to show myself around. I did not know it had been such a chore.'

'You think I say it is not right because being with you is a chore?' His voice seemed to echo off the sand dunes. He reached out his hand for hers, his thumb slowly beginning to draw hypnotic circles in her palm, shaking her to the core. 'It is not right because…because when I am with you I wish to kiss you. When we are in public, propriety prevents me, but when we are alone—'

She looked up at him, her eyes growing wide, her stomach doing somersaults.

'When we are alone, *kalilah*, I have to rely on my own self-control.'

He made it sound like a curse, but something in Tamara

was soaring obliviously, her arms reaching playfully around his neck, one corner of her mouth lifting into a daring smile. 'I thought self control was your forte.'

'I thought so too—' his voice was almost a groan that sounded like defeat as he guided her body closer '—until I met you.'

Unable to tear her eyes away from him, Tamara watched as his liquid brown gaze dropped to her lips and then, suddenly, decisively, his mouth followed. But the moment it did she was unable to focus on anything. Because if she thought Qwasir had surpassed her wildest expectations it was nothing compared to the long-awaited sensation of his mouth on hers. Gently exploring, testing, the tip of his tongue finding hers and flicking over it, teaching her the true meaning of anticipation. A feeling so new and so longed for that she wasn't sure she ever wanted it to end.

Until something brought her back to where they were. The sound of hooves. On sand. Approaching. Suddenly Kaliq let go of her and stepped back as if he had just discovered she was infected with some contagious disease. Tamara spun round to see his aide on horseback, squinting through the sliver of sunlight from a distance.

'Forgive me, Your Highness,' he called, stilling at the point they must have come into view, 'I missed you leaving and then…when I saw Amir I thought perhaps you were in trouble.'

'No trouble, Jalaal, thank you.' His voice was husky but level.

Jalaal nodded and turned without question.

Tamara frowned as Kaliq moved towards Amir. So he had *not* instructed his aide to leave them alone on purpose, and he certainly hadn't dismissed him on her account now. No, he fully intended to leave. Tamara drew in a ragged breath. Was Jalaal discovering that the crown prince had human desires like anyone else so terrible? Was desiring her so regrettable full stop?

'Don't tell me, Kaliq, it is *right* that we should be getting back.' Her voice was sarcastic. 'After all, tomorrow I'll be gone.'

Kaliq looked at her blankly. Down at the sand beneath his feet. Then out at the round sun shimmering on the horizon.

Like a gem.

Then suddenly a look came over his face unlike any she had ever seen before. As if he had just been handed a key to a door without a keyhole, and he wasn't entirely sure whether to leave it be or barge the door right down.

'Well?' she asked, her hands on her hips, looking at him and then at Amir.

And then he turned back to her quickly, as though her impatience had made up his mind.

'Tamara, will you marry me?'

Tamara stared in disbelief at the doubtful expression on his face and half-laughed, wondering if she had missed the joke.

'Marry you? Why? Because your aide just caught us alone together?'

Kaliq's mouth hardened. 'No.'

'Then why?' she asked softly, her voice barely more than a whisper.

'You wish me to list the reasons why? Is it not obvious?' He flexed his hand, then closed it again. 'Because you are exceptionally beautiful, and a virgin. Because you are the daughter of the ambassador, and you have shown great respect for my country in your own right. And because—as you know—I must marry in order to inherit the kingdom.' He paused as if to be sure there was no reason he had omitted and, to her consternation, she realised it was the first time in the last ten minutes she had seen him look utterly certain—there was not. 'Is that clear enough?'

'Perfectly.' Tamara felt as if her heart were a hologram and with the rising of the sun the light had made it cease to exist completely. For in one succinct sentence he had just listed all the reasons why she might be a suitable future queen, but none of the reasons why he might want her to become his wife.

Suddenly she knew that they had been worlds apart all along.

The truth was that this week had been a test of her suitability. It had nothing to do with encouraging her to pursue her dreams or to defy expectations—it had been a double bluff. He had cared about nothing but his precious duty all along.

And though she had fallen for him, though to say no would be to lose the one thing that had ever made her feel truly alive, to say yes would be to sacrifice the life she had only just begun to live. For how could she spend the rest of it trapped in a marriage to a man who didn't love her? That could only ever end the way her parents' marriage had—with a painful and bitter divorce splashed across the newspapers.

'Well?' he said, mocking her earlier impatience. 'What do you say to wearing the sapphires, Tamara?'

Tamara took a deep breath. 'I can't marry you Kaliq.'

Kaliq straightened indignantly as the sun rose high above their heads, the mystical glow of half light beginning to fade away.

'May I ask why?'

Is it not obvious? She wanted to retort in kind, but her pride forbade her. For how could she reply that it was because he did not love her, when to admit she loved him—when she had only known him for one week—was crazy. As ridiculous as saying yes to a man who had only proposed because she was the virgin daughter of an ambassador, and because he needed a wife in order to inherit his kingdom. And how better to escape the real reason than to answer as if she had simply been offered the job of queen, rather than asked the one question in the world that ought to have been motivated by love but which held none at all?

'Because I wish to be free,' she whispered brokenly, 'to live my life out of the spotlight yours attracts.'

Kaliq looked up from the final paragraph of the international trading treaty as the plane began its descent to his homeland, and his heart settled. It had consumed almost all his waking hours for the past few weeks and, finally, it was finished. He felt all the pleasure of a plan just as he had calculated—well reasoned and considered after days of deliberation—the way his plans always were.

Always, except once. His eyes roamed to Tamara, willing himself to feel the same sense of satisfaction as she sat there compliantly in exactly the way he had intended, but his mind only filled with scorn for his younger self. *That* idea then had come impetuously, irrationally, awkwardly. Had presented itself as an ill-timed but doable solution to satiate both his lust and fulfil his duty.

But then there had been nothing rational about his thoughts from that very first day he had met her, when he had known, unequivocally and inconveniently, that she was both innocent and the most desirable woman he had ever encountered. Less rational still had been that night when it had occurred to him that not only was she leaving, but that it was inevitable that on her travels she would meet some other man who would have no qualms about robbing her of her virtue. *He'd* wanted her, with an ache unlike any he had ever known. Yet to have taken her would have made him no better than some other man himself and, as a proud descendent of the A'zam tribe who had first civilised Qwasir, that had been out of the question.

Kaliq flicked open the lock on his briefcase. How much simpler the solution was now he knew that she had no moral code, he thought, gritting his teeth. How attractive the thought that after this week her face would never again pop into his head again during his discreet liaisons with the opposite sex, even if such escapades had ceased to satisfy him of late. In the same way that seeing her exposed on that billboard had put an end to those occasional, imprudent moments over the last seven years when he had wondered how things might have been different if he hadn't been born into the spotlight.

Now he knew that was irrelevant, as she would be, once he had her. For what could be more logical than a discreet, hassle-free and short-lived affair to finally put an end to the unfulfilled lust that damned photo had reawakened? Or more satisfying than to make her admit after all her protestations about seeking something out of the ordinary that she was just as desperate for fame, sex and money as the next woman?

She might pretend to be an anomaly to that same old formulae, sitting there, looking almost fretfully out at the view with her teeth gently nibbling on her bottom lip, making him feel like some kind of prison guard, but it was all an act. No doubt learned from her mother, whose fame she had pretended to detest.

Once she was his lover she would never be able to walk around with that semblance of innocence again. He would scorch the memory of every other man from her mind until he was etched irremovably on her brain. She would wear his jewels—once. Beg, cry out his name in regret. Then he would unclasp them from around her neck, and she would be gone from his life for good.

As the plane touched down expertly on the private airstrip, Tamara took a deep breath and swallowed down the lump that had risen in her throat, telling herself that opening that particular black box of memories was a good thing. For hadn't his behaviour during this journey alone gone some way to proving how her life might have been if she had answered him differently? Even if the hunger she felt just looking at him now proved that she hadn't succeeded in forgetting him as well as she'd hoped.

'You remember?'

His voice cut across the cabin and startled her out of her daydream. He was looking at her as she stared out of the window, her balled-up jumper inadvertently discarded as the plane came in to land.

'Yes, I remember,' she replied bleakly, still looking at the sand like spun gold as the sun beat down upon it, the majestic dark hills and the town a peppering of white dashes like some exotic Impressionist painting. Why hadn't she thought to harden herself against his homeland too?

As the plane came to a stop, he beckoned for her to stand and make her way to the exit.

'Much has changed since then, Tamara. Come.'

Did he suppose she needed reminding? Tamara stood up, avoiding his gaze.

'Indeed,' she replied bitterly as she turned her head to look out of the opposite window, where row upon row of vehicles were flanking the airstrip. 'For now it seems you require an entire entourage when you used to balk at all the fuss. Except an *aide*, of course.'

'I need no entourage.'

She laughed. 'What is this then—a desert park and ride?'

Tamara picked up her handbag and strode to the exit. He placed his muscular bronzed arm across her to release the door as she approached.

'*One* of those cars is a member of the palace staff waiting for us. Is that quite acceptable? Unless you'd rather walk, of course.' He looked distastefully down at her wedge shoes and small handbag. 'Do you happen to be carrying some factor fifty suncream, a pair of walking boots and ten litres of water?'

Tamara ignored him. 'What about the rest?'

'The rest, I suspect, are photographers.'

Tamara shook her head doubtfully. 'You *never* allow the press on royal territory.'

'As I said—' Kaliq swung back the door slowly '—much has changed, Tamara.'

He was bluffing, she knew it, and she had no intention of remaining in such close proximity to him whilst he taunted her.

Placing her bag on her shoulder, she stepped out of the aircraft. Suddenly the crowd below—like a colony of ants—swarmed into action, the sound of cameras filling the air. She shielded her eyes instinctively, sure she would never grow used to it.

'Smile, Tamara,' Kaliq drawled in her ear, coming up close behind her, 'even for you this must be exposure beyond your wildest fantasies.'

Tamara spun round, incredulous. 'Why? You hate the press!'

'I told you, my father is ill. As long as they run around making up lies about me, the less column space they give to him.' He looked at her intently. 'Even those you don't want close by forever have their uses in the moment, Tamara.'

'And let me guess,' she spat out venomously, 'this is my moment?'

'It's our moment, Tamara. Make the most of it.'

She almost lost her footing as the shocking, cruel parody of the words he had spoken rocked through her body. She stepped away from him instantly, the pack of photographers below suddenly the least threatening option.

'I don't want you, Kaliq.'

'Liar,' he ground out as he hauled her into his arms and carried her to the waiting Jeep.

CHAPTER FIVE

WASN'T it a hard and fast rule that something you remembered as huge and impressive from the past was inevitably small and unexceptional when you saw it again?

If it was, then whoever had said so had clearly never been to the A'zam palace, Tamara decided as the Jeep slowly reached a standstill outside the enormous Moorish entrance. For it seemed even more incredible to her now than it had done when she had seen so little of the rest of the world. Perhaps because now that she had, she no longer just *thought* it was more impressive than anywhere else—she knew.

Just like Kaliq, a voice inside her head taunted, forced to admit that, no matter what she had been pretending for years, no other man could compare to him. The insight made her throw open the car door and jump out before he had even killed the engine, anxious to escape the intimacy of the vehicle's interior. After that disquieting experience of being scooped up in his arms and held against his muscular chest, she'd spent the entire car journey making sure her legs remained as unlikely to brush against his hand as possible, and she had no intention of allowing her desire to run riot now.

If only she hadn't presumed he was bluffing about the damn photographers, been naïve enough to suppose that those heady summer days seven years ago meant she knew him. She didn't and, if his rebuttal of press intrusion had ever been real, then he *had* changed. Even if the impact of him—of this place upon her—hadn't.

Slowly and deliberately, Kaliq unfolded his lithe frame from the driver's seat and walked towards her, a flicker of amusement playing across his lips which told her that, despite the look of awe in her eyes, he knew her swift dash towards the palace gates had nothing to do with enthusiasm for the architecture.

'So *eager*, Tamara. Come.'

If he did remember the last time she had arrived, when he had found her in the dazzling marble atrium, then he allowed no flicker of recognition to cross his face as he led her through the entrance and purposefully across the floor. Her memories, on the other hand, made her feet so heavy she almost struggled to keep up with him.

But then why would he remember, when *every* woman he met wanted him? As he led her down one of the corridors, several female members of palace staff stopped to watch in admiration and bow as he passed. It irritated her more than it ought to have done.

'Is devoted adoration the main prerequisite when you recruit palace staff?' Tamara hissed sarcastically the minute they were out of earshot.

'Why, do you think you're perfect for the job?' Kaliq mocked.

'I'm afraid mute veneration isn't a look I've had much practice at.'

'Indeed.' Tamara saw Kaliq flex one hand and then relax it again. 'And, for your information, my staff usually pay little attention to my arrival—it's you who is the novelty.'

'Me?' she asked doubtfully. 'No one batted an eyelid the last time I was here.'

'Last time you were the daughter of an ambassador, not a *celebrity* brought here at my command to wear the matrimonial jewels.'

It ought to have been satisfying to have him, of all people, define her as something other than the daughter of one or the other of her parents, but his description only succeeded in shrinking her self-esteem to the size of a scarab beetle.

'I am quite sure they have seen you bring women back to the palace who are more famous than me, Kaliq.'

'On the contrary. I have never brought another woman here.'

If the words hadn't been spoken with such flippancy, Tamara might have melted a little at the romance in that. Or read something into the reason for such an ostentatious declaration, however false. But, the moment he said it, Tamara knew instinctively that it was true, and there was nothing remotely romantic about it. Kaliq was a man who kept work and sex separate. He would never let something as inconsequential as a woman impinge upon his royal affairs.

Which made her what, exactly?

'Your presence here is a business necessity,' he added, as if he had read her mind.

She wanted to yell back that she didn't suppose otherwise, that despite what people generally assumed about the size of models' brains, she didn't need everything spelled out for her, but before she got the chance he stopped so abruptly at an ornately carved rosewood door that she almost collided with the muscular body she had been taking such pains to avoid.

His eyes raked over her in savage appraisal. 'I like to keep a close eye on my investments, however temporary.'

The nearness of him did things to her insides and that made her even angrier than his words. 'If we have stopped because this is to be my cell during my sentence here, then please let me in.'

He arched one deprecating eyebrow as she looked hopefully at the door. 'I was just stopping to inform you that these are my father's quarters.' He looked up and down the length of the corridor and then back to the intricate entrance. 'This, in fact, is traditionally the marital chamber—' his eyes blazed into her '—not that you will ever have any need of this particular piece of palace geography.'

Tamara wished that the walls of the corridor would veer together and swallow her up.

'Just tell me where I'll be staying and leave me alone to…to get some rest.' Sleep was the last thing she felt capable of but she needed to put some distance between them, to attempt to build some kind of wall around her heart before her memories combined with his lingering musky scent that was most definitely in the here and now, and penetrated her heart irreparably.

'I brought you along this wing because my father wishes to see you as soon as possible. But if you wish to make him wait…'

Tamara looked horrified, as much at the possibility that she might offend the King as at the discovery that she was not going to be able to keep the low profile she had hoped for.

Kaliq's eyes dropped critically to her cropped jeans and fitted blouse. 'On second thoughts, perhaps it would be better if you changed first. We will dine at seven-thirty. In the meantime, Hana will take your measurements and show you to one of the guest rooms.' He nodded to somewhere behind her and a young Qwasirian woman who looked to be about Tamara's age stepped forward deferentially.

'And where is this guest room—as far from the royal quarters as possible, no doubt?'

'On the contrary, Tamara, it is next to mine.'

* * *

Tamara held out her arms stiffly as Hana flitted around her with a tape measure, telling herself it didn't make a blind bit of difference whether there was one door or a hundred separating her from Kaliq, because she was staying behind it whenever this assignment didn't require her to be elsewhere.

But the once clear perception she had had of those requirements seemed to be getting more diluted by the second, she thought, recalling his announcement that his father wished to see her as soon as possible. Was the King meeting everyone else involved in this royal gala as a matter of protocol, when he was far from fighting fit? she wondered doubtfully. Perhaps he simply wished to ask after her father. And what would she say? *Even though he has retired back to Britain, I see about as much of him now as I did at nineteen?* Tamara shook her head, recalling how he'd yet again declined her invitation to come along to the function she'd helped Mike organise last month.

Still, she thought, dragging her mind back to the present, fielding questions about her parents would be preferable to having to suffer the intimacy of dinner alone with Kaliq, and on the couple of occasions when she had met King Rashid previously he had made her feel truly at ease.

'I have finished, miss.' Hana stood before her with her head bowed respectfully, and Tamara realised that her arms were still outstretched as if she were walking some imaginary tightrope. She dropped them.

'I have prepared some fresh oils for you, if you would like to bathe before your meal.' Hana smiled as she motioned through to a room of gleaming white before bowing and moving to the door.

Snapping out of her daydream, Tamara followed Hana's

line of sight, astonished by the young woman's obvious pleasure in her work.

'That is very kind, thank you.'

She watched her leave, suddenly humbled by Hana's contentment and ashamed of her own melancholy. Had she any right to feel so wretched when, on the face of it, she was being given what to many girls would be a dream come true—being measured for a couture gown to be worn alongside the A'zam jewels? No, she hadn't, so she should just get on with it.

Tamara wandered across to the bathroom, deciding it was as good a place as any to divert herself, but as she entered the room it captivated her of its own accord. A level of comfort tended to come as standard whilst on location with the Jezebel team, but this was something else. She looked at the inviting sunken bath and the row of bottles beside it, each one filled with oil and petals afloat in different shades. She picked up one that was a translucent orange and lifted the lid. It smelled enticingly of ginger and juniper. She looked at her watch. When was the last time she had actually taken time out to really stop and relax? On the last couple of shoots she had barely had time to fit sleep into the equation. As for her days off, she had spent the last few walled up with Mike working out how best to use the extra funds. Before that…before that, she suspected she had *found* things to fill any time which might have allowed her a chance to reflect too deeply.

Annoyed at the realisation, Tamara made a pact with herself that for the next half an hour she wouldn't ponder anything at all except the incomparable restfulness of hot water on her body. Then she poured a generous swig of liquid into the tub and turned the tap on full.

* * *

An hour later, as she walked back down the corridor that Kaliq had so clearly identified as King Rashid's quarters, Tamara had to wonder whether allowing herself to think of nothing but warm water on skin had been the best idea. Although sinking down into the steaming tub filled with the relaxing and revitalising oils Hana had prepared had cleansed her mind and prevented her from analysing the events of the last twenty four hours, it had also succeeded in making her body ultra-sensitised. So that even when she'd wrapped herself in the fluffy white bathrobe afterwards, she'd wondered whether sometimes—if everything had been different—Kaliq might have slipped below the water with her and cradled her against his chest, run his hands over her breasts, tasted her neck with his lips.

Tamara shook herself and smoothed down the blue and white kaftan she was now wearing over soft blue loose fitting trousers. No, that was just a fairy tale. The kind of thing that married couples did in the movies, but no one actually did for real. She could barely recall her parents being in the same room as each other on two occasions in the same week, let alone showing each other any kind of affection. Though over the years her pessimistic attitude towards marriage had grown more realistic, she knew that if she had said yes to Kaliq, the whole thing would have probably been one long bath gone cold, waiting for a man who never came home, and when he did his mind and his heart would have been elsewhere.

Yet as she reached the door to the royal dining room, that photo of Sofia and Rashid kept popping into her mind. The one where Sofia looked incomparably content. Even her mother hadn't looked that happy in her wedding photos and she had been an actress, for goodness' sake. Sofia wouldn't have looked like that unless she had been sure that the man she was marrying had a capacity for love as well as the ability to be a great king. But that didn't mean her husband had necessarily passed both those skills onto his son.

Suddenly the door opened and Kaliq appeared, the sight of him in his eastern garb like an explosion of flavour in her mouth.

'His Highness will see you now.'

Not *my father*, she noticed, glad of the chance to focus on his telling choice of words rather than her nipples peaking at the sound of his voice. Was that damned oil some kind of aphrodisiac? She couldn't remember if that was one of the properties of ginger or not, but she blamed it anyway.

He led her through what she soon discovered was an anteroom, impressive enough in itself, then onwards to a larger dining room, decorated in regal shades of deep burgundy and gold with a table of rosewood at the centre that matched the intricate doors of the royal wing. At first she almost did not recognise the frail man who stood to welcome her but, as he took her hand in his cool grasp, a familiar smile lit the creases at his eyes. She lowered her head naturally, as much because of the wisdom and dignity he exuded as because he was the king of an illustrious desert kingdom.

'Please sit, my child. It is a pleasure to see you again.' Rashid's eyes brightened and the wrinkles on his face grew smoother, like a calming sea. 'With time, you have only grown more beautiful.'

'Thank you.'

As she took her seat beside Kaliq, a maid entered with three small glasses of a golden liquid.

'How is your father?' he said, smiling benignly. 'Still enjoying his retirement?'

'I believe so, yes.'

'One of the benefits of a job you choose as a career, rather

than one you were born into for life.' He c̶̶̶̶̶, ̶̶̶̶̶̶
wistfully for a second before continuing. 'I wis̶̶̶̶
for asking to see you on the same day that you have
here, and before you have even had chance to eat.' He ̶̶̶̶̶ed
as if the notion displeased him. 'But as Kaliq may have
informed you, my health is a little…changeable, and I wished
to thank you in person as soon as I could.'

'Thank me?'

Until now, she had to admit that she had not really considered what her visit meant to the King.

'We are exceptionally grateful that you have returned for
this event of Kaliq's.' He looked at her but gestured at his son.
'Your presence will assure the people of Qwasir that we are
a forward-thinking country, but with roots worth hanging on
to. It is a demonstration that, although things change, as
people we remain the same.'

Really? Tamara thought to herself, for hadn't Kaliq—who
she had once thought so open-minded—changed beyond all
recognition? But her heart was almost too full to wonder,
because King Rashid's poetic description of her purpose here
had suddenly made her proud and, more importantly,
reminded her that there was something larger at stake.

Tamara took a sip from her glass, the fiery taste a cross
between aniseed and cinnamon. The minute she swallowed,
warmth began to hum through her veins and she was suddenly
very aware that it was a long time since she had eaten. But
before she had time to politely request a glass of water instead,
she noticed Kaliq was looking at her expectantly, as if waiting
for her to respond to Rashid.

'Do people remain the same? An interesting question,' he
shot out abruptly, as if he had grown bored of waiting for her.
'Do experiences alter the way people act, or are people born

a certain kind right from the start, I wonder? It is that age-old question of nature and nurture, is it not?'

Despite posing it as a question, he looked at her with such derision it was obvious he had already made up his mind.

'A certain *kind*?' Tamara replied in disgust. 'I once met a man so open-minded he would have considered it a felony to tar all people with the same brush. I can therefore only conclude that experience does indeed change a man.'

'Oh, to be young and so impassioned by philosophy,' Rashid interrupted, chuckling softly. 'Please, do not let me crowd your debate. Much as I would love to join you for dinner, I must retire. Besides, it is only right you two are alone.'

He began to rise unsteadily from his chair, using the table for support.

'Father!' Kaliq sprang towards him, concern clouding his eyes, the cold austerity within them suddenly dispersed.

'I am perfectly capable of making my way to my own chambers, Kaliq.'

'Well, then, have the grace to allow me to feel a little capable too,' Kaliq replied slowly as he moved in, looking un-characteristically powerless.

As Kaliq led his *father* out of the room, Tamara stared into her glass for what seemed like an age. She felt humbled, and strangely empowered by the King. Not just by his words of support, but by his courage and humility. No wonder Sofia was smiling in that picture, she thought.

But after that little exchange it wasn't so easy to believe that Kaliq was entirely hard-hearted either. He might not always call Rashid *father*—but the moment he had done had been revealing. That was far less empowering. On the contrary, it weakened her defences.

'My father is a proud man.'

Kaliq re-entered the room, the sight of him causing a shiver to whisper down her body like cool summer rain.

'I imagine most truly great men are,' she said slowly, feeling something dangerous open inside her. 'May I be excused now?'

'Excused?'

'Since your father is unable to dine with us, I thought perhaps I might leave.'

'Is the idea of sharing food with me alone so repellent?'

If it was, then leaving this chair would be easy, she thought.

'Surely it cannot be proper for you and I to dine alone?' she tested, remembering how his aide had acted like their shadow the last time she had been here, hoping she might convince him to *make* her leave, because she wasn't sure she was capable of making herself.

'As my father said, much has changed.'

'Your customs have grown less archaic?'

'If by that you mean less proper, then no, that has not changed. It is you who have changed Tamara. For I would not dream of dining alone with you if you were innocent. But we both know you're in no danger of that.'

The minute he had finished his sentence the door opened and in walked three waitresses carrying hot plates of steaming food. She ought to have retorted with a snide comment that just because appearance played an important part in her job didn't mean she jumped into bed with anyone who asked her, but instead his words only seemed to set her mind wondering about just how many desirable and experienced women he had done more than dine with alone.

'Talking of experience…tell me, what else have you been up to since I saw you last Tamara? You travelled in Europe? Went to university?' He curled his lip as if the thought amused him.

Tamara didn't look up at him but dug her fork into a chunk of meat from the array of small dishes that the waitresses had set out in front of them. No doubt the experienced women he was used to dating usually refrained from all but a side plate of salad, but she didn't do dates—not that this was one—and, contrary to popular belief about models, she most certainly didn't do *not eating*.

'I travelled for about six months, yes, then studied languages—Spanish and French mainly. I had more jobs than I can remember—translator, tutor, PA.' She shrugged.

Kaliq looked at her, mildly surprised. He had had some vision of her working in bars and clubs in the back streets of London, waiting for someone to spot her as the next big thing. The knowledge that she had studied and had a host of other jobs that were perfectly respectable didn't seem to fit with the image he held of her. Though, come to think of it, she would never have had to have waited to be spotted—the first man she approached would have known he could sell any product he wanted if he pasted her mouth-watering half-naked body on the box. But it didn't change the fact that she was doing it now. That she had decided upon modelling as a whim only made her fickle to boot.

'And what, this job—' he gestured at her body as if modelling was a dirty word '—is the only one that, what is that phrase you have—floated your boat?'

She looked down. 'Something like that.'

'And you live alone?' He made it sound shameful.

'Yes, Kaliq—how revolutionary!'

He tutted. 'And, rather than settling down, men just come and go as it pleases you?'

'I don't wish to discuss my personal life.'

'Because it is no doubt just as changeable as the rest of

your life, which is precisely why a marriage between us could never have worked.'

Tamara felt as if someone had just kicked over her heart and dribbled it a hundred yards.

'And what of you, Kaliq? Have you even had time for anything but the *un*changing catalogue of royal duties?'

He raised his eyebrow suggestively. 'All work and no play is never the recipe for success. At least we agree on that. Just as we both seem to agree on pleasure for pleasure's sake.'

Tamara blinked down at her plate and laid down her fork, not daring to allow herself to look up, let alone process what he seemed to be intimating.

'It was a delicious meal.'

'You think I wish you to pretend that you do not know exactly what it is I am talking about?'

Tamara felt herself colour as two maids entered, one to clear their plates, the other carrying an enormous basket of colourful and exotic fruit.

Kaliq turned to them. 'Thank you. That will be all.'

Quickly, they departed. Kaliq fixed his eyes upon her once more as she twirled her empty glass between her fingers.

'Put down the glass, Tamara.'

He rose, the sound of the chair on the marble floor startling as he moved towards her, coming to rest onto the edge of the table just a few inches from where she was sitting. Her hands felt like someone else's in her lap, and she wondered if she ought to sit on them to stop herself reaching out to touch him. The powerful shafts of his thighs drew her gaze and she jumped embarrassingly as he reached across her to pick up a piece of fruit from the bowl in the centre of the table.

Then he looked at her with lethal decisiveness.

'You know I am talking about how much you want me, Tamara. About how much I want to take you to my bed.'

CHAPTER SIX

HE WANTED her.

Not because of her parentage or the catalogue of other bland merits he had once attributed to her. Not because of duty.

He wanted her because he was as overcome with raw, physical need as she was.

Maybe it was because he wanted to punish her. Maybe it would burn out after tonight. But though she might be lacking in technical experience when it came to sex, she knew enough about body language to be certain that the look of hunger in his eyes was real, that for once in his life he seemed oblivious to consequences, closer to losing control than she had ever seen him before.

That was fatal to her. Though she frowned and told herself it didn't change anything, her promise to keep this strictly business was already beginning to work its way out of her body with every breath she exhaled.

He looked irritated by her expression of torment, slowly moving the piece of fruit he had selected between his hands.

'Do not grimace as if I am making some loathsome demand, Tamara. Your come-to-bed eyes have been dissecting my body all evening. In fact, I'd hazard a guess that what you really want is to be wearing nothing at all, making a few demands of your own.'

Tamara blushed at her obviousness; she, who had made a career out of portraying emotions and had failed at indifference when it mattered most. Or did it? For wouldn't making love to him put an end to the unfinished business between them, once and for all?

She could invent a thousand justifications in support of it—and probably more against—but there was no point. Because her hunger went too deep, and the pledge to treat this like any other assignment was conveniently being replaced by an earlier promise to herself: to take every opportunity that came her way with both hands.

Slowly, resolutely she looked up and into his eyes of jet as her mind imagined what it would be like to run both those hands over his body, down the hard muscles of his arms, across the broad expanse of his chest, lower. Then came the sound of her chair scraping on the floor as she rose, just as unhesitant as his had been.

He moved before her, his hand snaking around her back to encourage her bottom onto the edge of the table, his body tantalising close.

'Close your eyes,' he whispered. Her body wound itself so tight in anticipation it was almost painful. She could sense him coming closer. 'Now taste it.'

The fruit was succulent and sweet and she bit into it uninhibitedly, swallowing hard. She felt the juice run over her chin and opened her eyes, raising one finger to catch the droplet of juice, but his hand reached out and encircled her wrist, deftly lying her back on the table before she had the chance, the half-eaten fruit with its pinkish-red flesh falling to the floor without either of them noticing. He leaned into her, his face so close to hers that she was shuddering with anticipation.

'It is called a quava. It's unique to Qwasir—you won't experience it anywhere else.'

Damn right she wouldn't.

She closed her eyes and almost cried out as his lips slowly began to kiss away the juice from her neck, pausing for just a second before finding her mouth. He explored it thoroughly, expertly. Every part of her felt as if it was holding its breath, ready, waiting, opening at the searing heat of his tongue. Each powerful, slick stroke seemed to reaffirm the curse she had feared all along, that for her there was only one man who could unleash feelings like these. Him. But as she felt the hand that had gently restrained her wrist make a tantalising journey to find the swell of her breast straining against the thin fabric of her kaftan whilst the other headed towards the moisture flowering between her thighs, it felt like a blessing.

Kaliq felt the tension in his shoulders gradually begin to skulk away like an animal banished as he possessed her mouth. He reached easily beneath the waistband of her flimsy trousers, lower, until he found her slick wetness beneath what he was surprised to find felt distinctly like plain cotton panties. The unexpected discovery—he would have put money on brazen silk or lace—only fuelled his erection. He wondered if he had ever been so hard. But then never before had he found the only woman who had ever told him *no* spread so wantonly before him that it wouldn't take much more to send her shuddering body over the edge screaming *yes*.

Was she always this responsive? he wondered angrily as he watched her blue eyes grow dark in pleasure.

'I want you, Kaliq,' she whispered softly, her hand clutching at the waist of his robes as he continued to touch her.

He imagined that hand between his legs and knew suddenly that if he continued a moment longer, in the next he would be plunging into her on the royal dining table. The thought was as arousing as it was responsible for shaking him back to the present. Because he was close to losing control and that wasn't part of his plan. He prided himself on control, it was in his blood as it had been in his ancestors' for thousands of years. Succumbing so soon would be a weakness, and though his body screamed to let go, his pride demanded retribution.

Kaliq reached out his hand to place it on top of hers.

'And you tried so hard to convince me you wanted nothing of the sort.' His voice dripped sarcasm.

'I was wrong,' she breathed, the absence of his hand at the most intimate part of her and its small, rhythmic movements—so new to her—was excruciating. She brushed her lips against his, coaxing.

But they met only with the cool air of rejection.

'We can't always get what we want,' he said grimly, backing away.

Tamara disentangled herself from him and sat up straight on the table, the blood rushing to her head. Was he actually stopping this, when it had been he who had spelled out so plainly the way in which they *both* wanted this evening to end?

Her eyes blazed with all the fury of a woman scorned and it ought to have satisfied him, but for some reason it only irritated him more.

'I have other business to attend to this evening.'

He took a step towards the door, looking so infuriatingly immaculate she could well believe he was capable of addressing the world's leaders at an earth summit and no one would guess what he had been doing only moments before.

She looked down, feeling suddenly cheap as her hair hung tousled around her face, her cheeks scarlet, the waistband of her trousers twisted at her hips and her top askew. Hell, she hadn't even stopped to consider that they were in the heart of the King's quarters and anyone could have walked in.

'Of course, Kaliq, heaven forbid I should interfere with your *duty*. That is, after all, why I am here.'

'I couldn't have put it better myself. Perhaps one evening when work is less *pressing* we will finish what we started. Perhaps not. But since you thrive on inconstancy, what could be better?'

That night she slept even more fitfully than the night before. It had felt like a walk of shame back down the corridor, past the door to his room, which filled her with loathing on sight, and into her own. Perhaps she ought to have felt grateful that she hadn't run into Hana or any of the other palace staff, or comforted herself that this was better than sleeping with him and then spending the rest of the week regretting it, but somehow it felt worse.

Because what kept her awake was how foolish she had been to suppose he'd wanted her with the wild abandonment with which she had wanted him. Yes, the hunger in his eyes and the daunting press of his erection against her stomach had been real enough, but his desire hadn't been a sign that he was losing control—it was a weapon fashioned to humiliate her in the worst possible way.

There was no comfort to be had in telling herself she could try and salvage her dignity over the next few days by staying clear of him until this whole thing was over, because she had already lived up to his damning opinion of her. Though she would do everything in her power to save herself the sheer mortification of *finishing what they had started* should he test her again, it didn't stop the treacherous ache inside that wished he would do just that.

Hearing him return to his room in the early hours of the morning only made it harder. Was that why he had commanded that she sleep in the room adjacent to his? Had he known she would lie hopelessly in her bed, desperately searching for a cool stretch of sheet, tangling herself in the clammy covers to stop herself from getting up and going to him, crawling into his bed and pleading with him to make love to her?

Every night only seemed to grow worse than the last. Probably because she had yet again made a misassumption where he was concerned. Because while she awoke each morning, determined to remain stony-faced and avoid his company unless it was strictly necessary in preparation for the gala on Friday, the reality was she barely saw him at all. Instead, Hana instructed her that each morning she was to be taken by her personal royal driver to the A'zam Plaza in Taqwasir, the country's capital, where the gala was to be held. Her days were soon filled with rehearsals, lighting checks, dress fittings and make-up trials. Each night, at varying times and from varying sources, she would be informed that Kaliq was tied up in some business or other, and asked if she would care to take dinner alone in the roof garden, on the terrace, or in one of the dining rooms.

Invariably she opted to eat at the small terrace that led off from her room. Tamara told herself it was because it was the option that generated the least fuss, and not because the few times she did see Kaliq—other than when he dropped into the Plaza between meetings to issue instructions to the creative director—he was coming or going from his room next door.

If he said anything more than a cool good morning, it was

to make a comment equally mundane, and it seemed to Tamara that he had made up his mind she *would* never be more pressing than business. But it didn't stop her wondering, which in turn forced her to consider whether he might have been right about her thriving on inconstancy. Somehow, he had managed to pinpoint exactly the part of herself she didn't like to spend time examining. Which was why, ordinarily, she made sure any spare moment she had was filled with work for Mike.

At least that was a constant in her life and, as if to prove it to herself, when the director at the Plaza informed her that she wasn't required for the rest of the day at about eleven a.m. on the Thursday before the event, Tamara decided to take the trip she had been contemplating. It was against Kaliq's advice, of course, to wander outside the palace unaccompanied, but by now she didn't much care.

Tamara walked out into the square where her driver was waiting.

'You finish for the day, Miss Weston?'

'Yes, Yonas. I wonder—' she hesitated '—I wonder whether, rather than returning to the palace straight away, you might take me across into Lan?'

Yonas looked surprised. 'Whatever you wish, Miss Weston.' He nodded but didn't start the engine immediately.

'I…my father was fond of one of the villages just over the border,' she clarified. 'I wanted to see it.'

He turned the key in the ignition as if that made perfect sense. She didn't like to lie, even if it was only a little white one, but it was simpler this way.

Tamara had never visited Lan before, but she had first heard of it about eight months after returning from Qwasir, the January she'd come home from Europe and started her language course. She had just had her first French class—the first lesson ever in which she had truly appreciated what a blessing it was to have the chance to learn—and had headed to the tennis club to sign up. And that was when she had met Mike. He had just finished a match and was pinning up a poster about a fund-raising tennis marathon in aid of something called the Start-A-School Foundation. It had caught her attention immediately because of the picture—a school before a backdrop of desert. Immediately she recalled the soaring sense of delight she had experienced—so close to the surface with her own return to education—when Kaliq had taken her to that school in Taqwasir. An experience which had changed her own outlook for ever, however much those days with him were twisted in her mind by heartache.

She'd turned to Mike, who was fiddling with a drawing pin. 'You're raising money to build schools abroad?'

He nodded, smiling. 'I founded the charity a couple of years ago, and we just built that one in Libya. We need a couple of thousand pounds more and we'll have enough to build one in Lan, a small country I trekked through in my gap year, just over the border from Qwasir. Want to help?'

Tamara looked at him, unequivocally certain of her answer. 'Yes, yes, I do.'

She and Mike had been firm friends ever since, and over the years they'd visited a couple of the schools they'd helped fund, including one in East Africa and one in Sierra Leone, where he'd met his wife Tia. With its close proximity to Qwasir, Tamara had had little desire to go to Lan, but now that she was staying only sixty miles west, it seemed silly to waste the opportunity. Especially considering it was the first school she'd help raise funds for, and Mike had been keen to send someone over to see whether the classes were as over-full as he feared.

The journey took just over an hour, and though the drive was smooth and her eyes heavy after another night of broken sleep, the scenery was so awe-inspiring that she stared out of the window in delight for the duration of the journey. Eventually, after they were allowed through border control on day passes and driven past an impressive mountain range bathed in midday sun, they stopped outside a row of interconnecting huts the colour of sandstone.

'Thank you, Yonas, here will be fine.'

She spoke to a young woman in the entrance hall and asked if she might watch for just for a moment. The woman nodded and proceeded with her to a classroom of what looked to be about sixty young faces following their teacher intently as he shared his knowledge. It stirred within her the same feeling that seeing such schools in progress always did: utter humility. The way she had felt in Taqwasir seven years ago when Kaliq had shown her the school, the final one Qwasir had needed to guarantee that no child had to travel more than walking distance to learn and that no class would ever be overcrowded.

Here, on the other hand, it looked as if Mike's suspicions had been right.

'Are all the classes of a similar size?' she tactfully asked the young woman.

'For now, yes. But a second school will soon be built a few miles from here,' she said proudly.

Tamara did a double take. The leader of Lan was well known for having no desire to spend money on his country's education, and she and Mike hadn't made any firm plans to build here yet.

'Your leader will fund a new school?' Tamara enquired hopefully.

The woman shook her head and smiled proudly. 'No. The crown prince of Qwasir has made the arrangement.'

Tamara wished she had never gone to Lan. It was typical that the one thing she had done to make herself feel better had only succeeded in making her feel worse. Because now she knew Kaliq was responsible for something that was so close to her own heart it was impossible to despise him. Of course, seeing the school he had founded in Taqwasir had been responsible for cementing her affection for the cause in the first place, but that was different. That had been part of his duty as the future leader of Qwasir. Building a new school in Lan went beyond his duty, and tonight would have been a million times easier if she had never discovered it.

As Tamara slipped on the impossibly high silver stilettos, she stood up straight and told herself to forget it. For the last three hours she had been pampered and preened by so many different people—the hairdresser, the make-up artist, her assistant, Hana, and the dressmaker—she'd had little else to do but allow her thoughts to wander. But, now she was alone, she needed to prepare for the task in hand.

Hana had informed her that palace security would bring the sapphires along any minute and she needed to feel nothing when she saw them. In exactly the same way that she gave no thought to whatever clothes and accessories the Jezebel stylists thrust in her direction because it was work. After all, the sapphires ought to hold no meaning whatsoever, for he had followed his so-called proposal by offering them to her as if they were the sole reason she might wish to accept it, when they couldn't have been more irrelevant to her. But perhaps that was why the thought of wearing them now felt so torturous. Because like the proposal itself they ought to have been offered out of nothing but love, but he had tried to use them like a bargaining tool.

Tamara stepped in front of the mirror, hoping a preparatory glance might harden her heart against her image, which was to be the antithesis of everything she might have been, but it didn't. The peach light of the desert dusk pierced through the sheer fabric at the window, bathing her in a bright glow that brought out the platinum thread of the silvery-white dress that had been designed especially for the occasion, the delicate fabric skimming over her skin. The tumultuous mixture of emotions caused her complexion to take on a rosy glow, enhanced by the soft make up, so different from the sultry tones she was so used to seeing upon her eyes at a Jezebel shoot. It was simple, understated…exactly what she would have chosen if she had been dressing herself, and that had never happened before. Even the length of her hair—so often made to look darker, redder—was softly piled on her head, its autumnal shade somehow seeming all the more soft for it. *Like a bride on her wedding day*, she could not help but think as she lifted her hand to her throat, the acknowledgement of it startling.

'Something missing?'

The voice came out of such stillness that she wondered how long he had been standing there. He seemed to be making a habit of it—entering unnoticed and with what felt like almost planned irony, at that exact moment when she allowed an ounce of magic to take hold of her, just for a second. And now he was here, like some dark predator come to reaffirm his power, and it suddenly seemed obvious that he never would have denied himself the satisfaction of this moment. Let alone trust his precious rocks to another, she thought as she eyed the oblong wooden box he was gripping with dormant strength. Her back was still turned to him as she studied his reflection—marginally easier, but no less astounding. Other people's mirror-images always looked somehow unlike them; her own features were far from symmetrical, her mother's smile had always been more pronounced on one side. Not Kaliq Al-Zahir A'zam. His reflection only confirmed the perfect set of every feature on that regal face of his, each virile inch of his body proportioned and set with such symmetry that she might have been looking at a statue by one of history's greatest sculptors.

'Missing? I suppose the answer to your question depends upon whether you rely upon material wealth in order to feel complete.' Her curt tone was loaded with cynicism as the need to do anything but stand there passively took hold. 'I see you still haven't learned to knock.'

'Nor you to tell intruders to leave soon enough for them to believe you mean it.'

Kaliq was unable to drag his eyes away from her, and it irritated him. He had selected the design for that dress himself, with the right balance of simplicity and elegance to accompany the necklace in mind. Yet whilst he had visualised the soft, light fabric skimming her figure, his mind's eye had been nothing like the vision before him. It clung to her provocative curves, whilst her face looked…like the first day she'd arrived here in her school-girlish dress, radiating youthfulness. And though he knew it was just the skill of the make-up artist, she looked so unexpectedly vulnerable that he almost considered calling the whole thing off and sending her back home as if she were a pearl he had mistakenly detached from its shell.

Yet, equally, he wanted to drape the jewels around her neck in answer to her beauty, to feel her skin burn beneath the

touch of them, of him. To lock the door on the night, on
Qwasir, and possess her as he had longed to do—with even
greater intensity than before—since the night he had seen her
desire first hand, felt her burn beneath his touch.

But he hadn't brought her here purely for his pleasure, had
he? She was here to serve a purpose tonight—to remind his
people of Qwasir's eminence and to draw the world's eyes
away from his father's illness as only wealth and beauty could.
So why had the past few days spent trying to prove that felt
like self-inflicted torture?

Tamara watched in the mirror as he stroked the few strands
of her hair which had been left loose to one side, clicked open
the box and carefully placed the jewels around her neck. As a
royal husband would his wife, she thought, trying to focus on
the properties of the stones instead. They were heavier than
she had anticipated, but then they were the most valuable set
of sapphires on earth. She walked her fingers up her chest,
stopping just short of touching them. The colour was like
every hue of the ocean all at once, drawing the eye with such
intensity, yet boundless at the same time. She fixed her gaze
straight ahead with practised strength, remembering that *he*
placed them there without any of the freedom or love they
were supposed to represent.

'You look faultless.'

Faultless. The word bounced unevenly around Tamara's
mind like a rugby ball—one moment she deplored its indeci-
pherable meaning, the next she was dangerously aware that
it sounded as if it was spoken with the same honesty as when
he had told her he wanted to take her to his bed. But she
couldn't have got *that* more wrong.

'Faultless?' she asked quietly, attempting to keep her
voice level.

The muscle in his jaw tensed, as if she had reminded him of something unpleasant. 'One compliment not enough for you, Tamara? You wish me to continue—whet your appetite for the evening's exposure?'

'You think I care what the world thinks of me?'

Kaliq looked thoughtful. 'That would be ironic—' he laughed '—to offer yourself up for the world's critical appraisal if you did not care, yet why would you offer yourself up, unless you care for nothing else?'

'And what of the irony of you, Kaliq? You lecture me about caring what people think, when this whole evening is about engineering people's thoughts.'

'It is for my people's own good.'

'Really? Are you sure it is not for your own good, Kaliq?'

His eyes raked over her. 'I can assure you if this was about me we'd be going nowhere right now.'

'And what if this was all about me?'

'Then you'd be in heaven,' he drawled, as if she were a child who was only satisfied if everyone was looking in her direction.

'Would I indeed?'

'Yes. Because if this was all about you I'd take you through to the bedroom and you would never want to come out,' he said as he dropped the searing heat of his lips to her own momentarily before ushering her out of the door.

CHAPTER SEVEN

As Tamara stood backstage at the A'zam Plaza watching for her cue, she tried to remember what usually ran through her mind moments before stepping into a room full of people waiting for her to appear. Surely nine times out of ten she wasn't wishing she could click her fingers and disappear beneath the floor, leaving nothing but her couture dress—and in this case the sapphires—in a pile on the floor?

She cast her mind back to her few appearances as the Jezebel girl at product launches and the couple of catwalk shows she had done for Lisa's collection. She was convinced that, more often than not, she would be wondering about something as trivial as what to have for dinner after the show. But when she thought about food in an attempt to distract herself tonight, it only brought back memories of how he had fed her that succulent fruit with his fingers, and that was even more dangerous than giving in to her nerves. Nerves which normally didn't affect her, the way she'd never been afraid of spiders, or flying, because until this moment she had always felt the eyes of the audience weren't really on *her*, but on whoever she had been asked to be.

But tonight it didn't feel like work, or that she was playing someone else at all. No, tonight when she had looked in the mirror she had seen herself and, after that episode in her room, there was no forgetting that this was as much a moment in her personal life as it was in her career. It felt like stepping out wearing her own face, and that was as scary as falling out of the sky without a parachute.

Only because you're making yourself feel that way, she derided herself. *Don't give in to it; that's precisely what he wants you to do.* Resolutely she pursed her lips, sensing the fresh lipstick she had hastily reapplied in the car. Praying that no one would notice that they were still swollen from the heat of his kiss.

His anger perplexed her. She had expected him to gloat, for tonight was, after all, why he had flown halfway round the world to claim her as if she were the stand he needed for his priceless Fabergé egg. But somehow she had still managed to displease him. Maybe she ought to have felt gratified by his dissatisfaction, but it only annoyed her that nothing she did ever reached his ridiculously high standards. Was that why he had never married anyone else? she wondered, but then decided that even speculating about that was an extremely bad idea.

Just think about tomorrow, she told herself, staring up at the chic walls, all pale apricot panels and cream inlays. Tomorrow, when she would be on the plane home, when this would all be over. Yet that day seemed as if it was written into someone else's schedule, not her own. Was that because he had suggested—even if only to unnerve her—that sex *was* on the cards all over again?

'You're on, Miss Weston.' The visual director nodded, snapping her out of her wayward thoughts.

Tamara had practised the circuit around the gallery of the unique ballroom-cum-theatre and through the centre of the room to the stage so many times in the last few days that she ought to have been able to walk it with her eyes closed, but as she stepped out she realised that no rehearsal could have prepared her for this. It suddenly felt nothing like a catwalk and everything like an endurance test. But not for all the reasons she might have expected—the vast number of people and cameras, the fear of tripping up in her gown, which hadn't been ready for the dress rehearsal, of not correctly timing her arrival on stage with the crescendo of the freshly composed music. It was because of the sight of Kaliq, standing in his royal robes at the end of the walkway.

He had changed. His *kandora* was dark blue—A'zam blue. His simple headdress matched. So many Arab men, she had noticed, seemed to look as if the robes were wearing them. Kaliq wore his with such proud arrogance they might have been a second skin, equally ready to greet some of the world's most elite or ride out into the wilderness of the desert to see off an enemy tribe.

It shook her to the core more deeply than it ought. His presence was *always* astounding and, having overlooked the impact of his title once in her life, she had promised herself that she never would be guilty of that again. But when they'd been arguing in a dressing room in London or dining alone in a room of the palace, it had still been all too easy to consider only what he meant to her and forget who he was to the rest of the world. Sheikh Al-Zahir A'zam: first in line to the Qwasirian throne.

However, the effect of seeing him look more powerful and elemental, more startlingly male than ever before, was nothing compared to the torrent of emotion as she turned and prepared to walk up the central aisle. Hideous irony washed over her in a wave. He was waiting for her at the other end. Guests on either side. The sapphires. A nightmarish imitation of what might have been. No doubt exactly as he had planned it.

For a moment she stopped and stood completely still, as if her heart sinking in her chest had taken down her entire nervous system with it. The crowd drew breath. Kaliq's eyes narrowed in displeasure, his face like granite. She closed her eyes. *Keep breathing. Keep walking.*

She felt like a fawn taking her first few steps, but the audience gasped in pleasure as if it had been an exercise in suspense. She fixed her eyes at the back of the stage and didn't look at Kaliq's face again. Dared not, for fear that moment of paralysis would become permanent.

She reached the stage in perfect time as the music reached its triumphal conclusion, and was grateful to find that standing beside him was marginally easier to deal with. Kaliq might be closer, but he was out of her line of sight. That was taken up by the paparazzi and the crowds she was better equipped to deal with. Even if every row looked like a *Who's Who* of world royalty, each glamorous woman ooh-ing and ahh-ing as their eyes darted hungrily between Kaliq and the necklace.

Kaliq raised his hand and the room immediately fell silent.

'Thank you. It gives me great pleasure to welcome you to Qwasir.'

The room filled with the sound of applause.

'This evening is a celebration of our country, and what better way to begin than with this exhibition of the A'zam Sapphires—a symbol of our deep and spirited history. We are honoured that Miss Weston consented to wear them for us tonight.'

Tamara felt her heart beating so loud she could hear it in her ears. Honoured? How magnanimous! And about as sincere as the smile she had pinned to her lips.

'Not only were the unique sapphires unearthed from

Qwasirian soil, but the necklace has remained an important part of Qwasir's heritage for centuries. And since this is an evening of looking to the future as well as celebrating the past, I would like to present a few select awards to people of our country whom I believe have been truly forward-thinking. First, may I welcome to the stage Ahmed Khan, who has turned the disused gem mine on the East Coast into a visitor centre, the revenue of which has been used to fund a new sports centre for children.'

More clapping filled the room as Kaliq reached across her to retrieve the award from the podium. 'To some people, tonight is about more than just the chance to appear on every front page in the world,' he murmured sardonically before smiling broadly as the camera zoomed in on him. For the first time it occurred to her that the job of projecting a certain image wasn't such an alien concept to him as he might have her believe.

Just as she wasn't quite the woman she would have him believe, she thought. What would he say if she whispered back that every penny he was giving her was going towards building schools like the one in Lan? Probably that it was all a publicity stunt, she thought. Because he thought he had her all worked out. And wasn't it safer that he did?

Yes, and safer still would be focusing on some of the inspiring people taking to the stage rather than on his disturbing presence beside her. Yet even that wasn't easy. When she had been told at rehearsals that he intended to present several awards, she had presumed that it would be to some long-standing dignitaries, not to ordinary people who had really made a difference, and to whom he clearly meant every word of thanks he uttered. It raised such a host of conflicting feelings inside her that, as Kaliq began to draw the awards ceremony to a close, she almost didn't notice the members of the press jostling in the front row until one voice shouted more loudly than the others.

'And what of the King, Your Highness? Is his absence tonight an indication that his ill health shall prevent him from being a part of Qwasir's future?'

Kaliq stilled, every eye on the room on him, waiting.

Tamara remembered a conversation her mother and father had once had—on one of the rare occasions they had been together in the same room without arguing—about how the rhetorical expertise required for both acting and politics were not so very different. But as Kaliq prepared to answer the question he could have chosen to ignore, she recognised that there was nothing practised about his pause. The skill of having the right words at the right time seemed to come as naturally to him as breathing.

'On the contrary, I am certain that my father's greatness will be felt in Qwasir for many centuries to come.'

'And is this unveiling of the sapphires a sign that you plan to marry soon, and guarantee your own place in Qwasir's future, Your Highness?'

'If you ask whether it is a sign that I will do my duty where Qwasir is concerned, as my family have done for centuries, then the answer is yes.'

Kaliq nodded to the orchestra then as the press broke into a frenzy of speculation amongst themselves.

Tamara's heart twisted. Of course he planned to marry soon. He would always do what was best for his country. In the past she had thought that unquestionably living up to his peoples' expectations was weak. Now, to her chagrin, she grasped the strength that took. The pressure, the sacrifice of having his personal life dictated by duty. Such a lack of

freedom went against everything she believed in and yet…
she admired him more than she had ever admired anyone else
in her life.

As the crowds began to disperse and make their way to the
bar, Tamara took a deep breath and felt the muscles which had
been buoying up her smile lose their fight. In the last ten
minutes she had not only been dragged through the emotional
wreckage of her dreams but, worse still, she had seen that the
Kaliq whom she had fallen for that summer did exist after all.
It had been easy to believe from the other side of the
Mediterranean, even across the corridor from his room, that
his arrogance and disrespect for anything but his precious
crown were despicable and that his allure was down to nothing
but his physical perfection. Much harder to reconcile was
standing beside him and witnessing what a remarkably noble
man he really was.

Tamara walked to the edge of the stage, her mind like a
washing machine on spin. She knew she was expected to mingle
amongst the guests but the need to take a deep breath of fresh
air and gather her thoughts was greater—just for a moment.

Kaliq began to circulate. The King of Lan's wife was chatter-
ing in his ear about the sapphires, but his eyes remained fixed
on Tamara. As every man's had from the minute she had
stepped out from behind that teasing curtain of fabric and
completed that agonising erotic circle of the room, he
thought. There had not been one person who had not been en-
thralled, and there could be no pretending it was the inanimate
jewellery that held their interest. He doubted if any man in the
room could have even told him the colour of the stones at that
moment. It was *her*. The photographers were so captivated
they almost forgot to take her picture, husbands tripped

forward, suddenly oblivious of their wives beside them, mesmerised and longing to get closer. And who could blame them? It was as if walking—hell, just being—was an art form only she had truly mastered. Cultivated to beguile every man in the room. It frustrated him even more now than it had done when he had walked into that godforsaken studio less than a week ago. Because tonight those lush curves were on display to the world at his damn behest!

Then he saw something that caused his anger to burst its banks. Like a satellite travelling disobediently off his state-of-the art radar, she suddenly disappeared from the periphery of his vision. Wearing the royal jewels.

The night air was cooler than she had anticipated. It reminded her of the Christmas she and Lisa had gone to Sydney to visit some old school friends several years ago—the temperature so unexpected it was like the weather had somehow lost its way, misplaced somehow.

But misplaced suited her mood, she thought, momentarily reflecting that each one of those friends had now married and settled, and here she was, alone in the middle of a country where she did not belong, no matter how much her heart protested otherwise. And even if she *had* had a purpose here momentarily, it no longer existed. Even though—

Even though she was in love with him. It was as simple and as complicated as that. And she no longer loved him in spite of who he was but equally well because of it. Yes, she loathed the way he had brought her here for revenge and rejected her body and soul, but when did the human heart ever take heed of reason? How could it, when it almost overflowed just watching him on that stage, disbanding reporters as one might brush away a fly, when they sought to expose his inner turmoil? For whilst on the one hand she recognised the cold and ruthless exterior of a royal heir to whom duty was primary, what inner strength he possessed at every turn!

Yet to suppose that she was alone in being attracted to that, to harbour the belief that if she could only get close to him she could somehow unlock him, was as foolish as agreeing to come here in the first place. When he spoke she had felt the awe of every woman in the room, had seen it still lingering in their eyes when she'd slipped away.

Mindlessly, she took another step away from the side of the Plaza and out of the light pouring through the fire escape, drawing in a deep breath. A slight shiver of trepidation ran over her, disquiet interrupting her breathing. It infuriated her that Kaliq's warning that she should not go out alone in Qwasir suddenly sprang to mind, yet instinctively she felt it was time to go back inside.

But, as she turned, the fire door through which she had come slammed behind her, taking with it the strip of light.

And in its place a figure shrouded in darkness. Poised for her approach. A flash of metal glinting in his hands.

Tamara's breath caught in her throat and instantly a wave of fear rocked though her. She vaguely recognised him as one of the men who had been brought in to move the stage equipment—burly, mute and someone she had supposed harmless. Now his expression was anything but. He stepped forward.

Her eyes darted from side to side, wondering which was the best route of escape. She played for time.

'What is it you want?' Her voice was desperate.

He grinned, showing a row of crooked teeth, and dropped his eyes. And suddenly she realised.

The sapphires.

For a moment she had actually forgotten she was wearing

them. God knew how. The realisation that he wanted the necklace terrified her even more. Whether he had been planning this or taking a chance because the airhead model had stupidly chosen to wander outside alone. The necklace was so valuable there would be nothing most criminals wouldn't stop at to get it, but there was no way she was going to play the pathetic damsel in distress. A fierce anger swelled inside her.

Fight or flight was not a conscious decision she made, but as she darted instinctively to the right she felt a body grab her from behind and an arm lock around her neck.

She screamed.

He wasn't working alone. It was ridiculous to close her eyes in fear but she couldn't stop herself. Tamara heard the sound of a blade being drawn from a sheath and forced her eyes open.

It was inches from her neck. One movement and either the string of sapphires or her throat would be cut. She might want to run but, if she couldn't, that left only one alternative. *Fight.*

How was not so obvious. She looked down at the ground, trying to think fast. Then it came to her. Quickly lifting her right stiletto, she stamped down as hard as she possibly could on the sandalled foot of her attacker.

As he wailed in agony, loosening his grip on her, she dropped. Like a bird out of the sky that had been shot, falling through his grasp and catching both men unawares. The blade caught her arm and blood came, stinging, scarlet and hot.

Capitalising on the distraction, she kicked off her shoes and gained a head start on them. She dared not lose a second by turning around to see how much. She could already hear them in pursuit, gaining ground, the sound heavy in her gut.

Until the footsteps were replaced by commotion: shouting in a language she couldn't understand and a horse whinnying. But she didn't stop. If there were more of them, if they caught up with her on horseback, then the chances were they would take her too far away for anyone to hear her scream, and no one would ever know what had happened to the jewels. She raised her hand to her neck, beset with the need to protect them, preparing to unclasp them…if she could make them think she still had them on her but toss them somewhere Kaliq might have a chance of finding them—

But as she raised her hand she suddenly felt an arm reach around her. Encircling her waist from behind, hauling her on to horseback with a vice-like grip. She fought, twisting and kicking her body every way she could think of, thrashing from side to side, when she caught the blurred sight of the two men falling away like skittles knocked aside.

And then it hit her.

Before her eyes even had a chance to see, her ears had a chance to hear, or her brain could decipher what was part of the attack and what wasn't, her heart knew.

The rider was Kaliq.

CHAPTER EIGHT

HE DIDN'T say a word.

Even though the terrified shouts of the men soon fell away and the only sound that remained was the rhythmic gallop of his stallion as they rode out into the darkness. Even though the second she had understood it was him, she had mounted the horse behind him and knotted her arms desperately around his waist.

Still he did not speak.

Tamara did not know how long they had been travelling; knew only that although the fear-induced adrenaline that was responsible for the double-quick tempo of her heart had finally begun to subside, her pulse remained just as fast. She breathed in deeply, her body pressing closer to his back, the exotic smell of him and of the desert almost inseparable. And dangerously arousing.

In that moment, clinging to him had been instinctive. Now that the danger had passed, it felt embarrassingly familiar. Her whole life, she had prided herself upon her independence, upon defying people's expectations. She had fought anyone who held the view that a woman needed male protection: most of all him. But, when it mattered, her proclamations of strength had proved empty. Tamara cringed; she had unthinkingly laid herself so open to attack that, without him to rescue her, she might never have escaped. Then she had bound herself to him as if she would cease to exist without him, and she had yet to let go. Kaliq, on the other hand, had proved his point *and* lived up to the reputation of every one of his fore-bears out here in the unforgiving desert—commanding more fear and demonstrating more power when put to the test than he exuded when ensconced in the luxury of the palace.

Mortified by her stupidity, and fearful that if she didn't loosen her grip around him now, she might never find the strength, Tamara forced herself to move. Uncomfortably, she ran her hand over her arm, her fingers finding the cut, dry with blood. She had forgotten, and momentarily it brought back the traumatic image of glinting metal in the darkness, the sordid smile of crooked teeth. Not a scene from some late-night tele-vision thriller, but her memories.

The movement seemed to register with Kaliq, and finally he spoke.

'You are hurt.' His voice was level, unreadable.

She shook her head. 'Not badly.'

He threw none of the accusations she expected: that she should have listened to him, that she had put the royal gems at risk, though surely it was because he had been watching *them* with all the attention of a hawk that he had noticed her step outside in the first place.

'I just needed to…escape for a moment,' Tamara said awk-wardly, feeling the need to explain all the more because he hadn't asked.

But no remonstration came. Instead, she thought the dark shadow of his head nodded in understanding, but she might just as easily have imagined it.

'They will be punished,' he said firmly, after several

minutes had elapsed. 'They shall face the consequences of their betrayal.'

Kaliq willed himself not to think of that now, of anything but the solace of the desert, the way he always did when he rode Amir, however infrequently he seemed to get the chance of late. But, no matter how much he willed it, the image of her crawling away from those goddammed outlaws, blood smeared across her pale flesh, wouldn't leave his brain. To the extent that, had he not forced himself to rein in his fury, he would have brought Amir to a standstill with the sheer tension in his legs.

Yet beneath that anger was an emotion he was far less experienced at controlling, that could not be appeased by the thought of the two swift arrests which he hoped his silent signal to Jalaal had put in motion when he had noticed that member of the backstage staff disappearing after Tamara. An emotion which he could devise no practical solution to placate.

Fear.

That what he had asked her to do had put her in danger, and he might so easily have failed to protect her. It wasn't the same unease as when the people of his country were at risk; he bore that like a great weight on his shoulders. This was more acute, like an arrow penetrating the contour behind his collarbone and sinking into his chest.

Even though tomorrow she would no longer be his concern. His mouth tightened. Letting go of a woman had never bothered him before. Was it because until the events outside the Plaza he had conceded that tonight it was time his desire was finally satiated, time for her to prove exactly what kind of woman she was…and now she had never looked more vulnerable?

But still he rode on. Further away from the royal celebrations. Deeper into the night.

Tamara felt Kaliq's shoulders go taut and, fearful that his silence might continue, said the first thing that came into her head.

'Where are we going?'

'Somewhere we almost went a long time ago.'

Now it was her turn to tense. She hadn't thought about it until then, but it was suddenly perfectly obvious where they were going, for hadn't she already sensed a certain déjà vu? The mountains coming into view, the same clear, albeit now pitch-dark view of the horizon. Kaliq was riding her back to the cavern in the middle of the desert. The one they might have entered had Jalaal not interrupted seven years ago. The one that had amazed her then because it seemed to appear out of nowhere, as it did now, as if by chance.

But Kaliq never left anything to chance.

'Come.'

Effortlessly, he dismounted the horse and, before her mind had time to process the command, he scooped her up from the saddle. Any ordinary man might have just offered her a hand, she thought as she fought to compose herself, but when had anything about Kaliq Al-Zahir A'zam ever been ordinary? He placed her down on the ground and she felt the coarse sand beneath her bare feet, though the ground had never felt less firm. She had no time to ponder the irony. He was already leading her to the entrance, the low, inconspicuous opening in the rock just visible in the moonlight.

There was no stopping outside, no hesitation—from him or from her. But, as she stepped through the door, she was taken aback. From the outside it looked like nothing more than a gap in the mountain, a natural shelter from desert storms for whoever was passing—shepherd, warrior, king. But inside it was even more breathtaking than all the rooms at the A'zam palace put together. Muted lamplight illuminated rich gold and orange Bedouin silks draped across the ceiling and walls. A richly textured carpet cushioned her feet. Each item of furniture was so intricately carved she could well believe each piece protected a secret of the past.

'Sit,' he commanded, motioning towards one of the low divans.

She sank down naturally as she gazed around her in awe.

'What is this place? I thought—' She didn't know what to think.

'It is the true resting place of the A'zam Sapphires.'

Tamara looked puzzled, unable to comprehend what he meant.

'When Qwasir went through a period of unrest during the fourteenth century and the ruler of Lan threatened to invade—' he looked appalled at the thought '—it was decided that the sapphires should be kept outside the palace.'

'So your family sought somewhere that no one would ever dream to look?' she asked, remembering the replicas that had been on display when she had first arrived. It hadn't occurred to her that the real jewels would be anywhere other than locked in some royal vault hidden deep within the palace walls.

'On the contrary. Legend has it that this place found the A'zam family.'

Kaliq frowned at his own words. He had not planned to tell her the story, had never recounted it to anyone, in fact, though he had thought about it often since his father had told him as a boy. He walked over to the opposite side of the room and opened one of the cabinets as he continued.

'On his wedding night, Salah, the crown prince at the time, rode his new bride into the desert so they might spend their first night together away from the palace as husband and wife.

Salah planned to take his wife to the oasis on the other side of the mountains, but not long after they had set out, an unforeseen sandstorm forced them to try and find shelter from the cutting winds. Legend has it that this gap in the rock appeared just as they were beginning to give up hope. It has been the secret of generations ever since. The A'zam nuptial chamber and a fitting resting place for the gems.'

Tamara's eyes warmed at the romantic tale of Kaliq's ancestors. Until the cogs of her mind began to apply this new information to what had occurred outside seven years before. Kaliq had stepped away from the entrance the minute Jalaal had seen them. Was it because he was ashamed that they had kissed, as she had always believed, or because this place was so secret that even his aide must not know of it? Perhaps it didn't matter. It didn't change the list of reasons for his proposal back then, however significant the location. Any more than the fact that they were together in this nuptial chamber meant anything now; she was only here because returning the gems to safety was his only concern, and they just happened to be attached to her. That it completed the hideous parody of walking down that aisle towards him earlier tonight was probably just an added bonus.

'You don't consider my knowing about this place a danger?'

He selected a saucer and a decanter full of dark amber liquid from the cabinet and turned back towards her, his eyes fixed on hers.

'You could have surrendered the sapphires to save your own life. You didn't.'

Why hadn't she? Tamara wondered, leaning back and catching sight of her torn dress, the dried stains of blood on her arm, her dusty feet. Because she believed in right and wrong and the sapphires didn't belong to a thief—they belonged here, with the A'zam prince. *As she did?* Tonight had begun with what *most* women her age would have considered the stuff of dreams but, after the nightmare in the desert, it seemed to be ending disturbingly close to dreams of her own.

Kaliq walked over and sat beside her on the divan, looking at her arm as he kicked off his shoes. He poured the transparent liquid into the dish before dipping in a cloth and wringing it out.

'You told me they did not hurt you.'

His voice was thick with anger, and the realisation that it was directed at the attackers for hurting her threw her out of kilter even more than the closeness of his body.

'I'm...'

Fine, she had meant to say, but the words did not come because he was examining her arm so softly with his finger-tips that the feather-light sensation set every nerve-ending in her body aflame. It was ridiculous that a simple gesture had such a profound effect. Ridiculous and intoxicating.

She winced only slightly as the alcohol met her cut, almost glad to focus on the physical pain rather than the slow, dull ache of need that was spreading through her limbs, making them heavy. But the distraction only lasted a moment because now he was gently moving the strap of her dress to gently cleanse her shoulder.

She watched his long, lean hands at work, mesmerised by their darkness against her pale skin. Healing hands, she thought. She remembered him telling her that he had studied medicine in Europe. What would he have been if his future had not been mapped out before he was even born? she wondered. A doctor, perhaps. Who might have allowed himself to fall in love with a woman, proposed because he wanted to be with her and not because he had a duty to fulfil? The ridiculous image of a couple on their wedding night popped into her head, wearing their faces. She banished them. Since when had *she* fantasised about marriage?

It was the events of the evening, the stories of the past, the temptation to believe that in this place he was somehow free from the constraints of the palace that was making her head spin. After all, the whole purpose of tonight had been political, and ending up here was about nothing more than the security of the sapphires. She watched as he wrung out the cloth into the saucer. It was time to break whatever spell she'd allowed herself to fall under.

She stood up, raising her hands to the weight of the necklace, finding the ancient clasp.

Instantly he registered her intention and rose to his full height before her. 'Don't. Leave them on.' His eyes burned into hers.

She lowered her arms. The spell remained intact.

He did not touch her, but she read on his face the same need that she had seen that night when he'd laid her down on the dining table at the heart of the royal palace. Only now they were here, and this time she understood. That he did not want to desire her, but he did. That the games were over and tonight he was waiting—no, needed—for her to admit with her body that she regretted ever turning him down.

And, greater than all of that, she understood that it was inevitable. For wasn't the attack an even greater reminder than the past to seize life with both hands? If she *didn't* move now, she would spend the rest of hers wondering whether she had made the wrong decision. Twice.

Slowly, her eyes leaving his, she slipped down the straps of her dress.

Kaliq watched as she revealed one perfect milky-white breast and then the other, feeling himself grow harder. He had waited for this moment, for her to come to him because if she didn't she would die of longing. And yet it was not as he'd expected. The action—which ought to have felt so forward—seemed unpractised, her big doe eyes so wide and questioning that if he hadn't known better he would have guessed she was innocent.

She reached her arms behind her back to try to undo the zip of her dress and he was mesmerised by the sight of her full breasts rising beneath the sapphires. Angrily, he remembered the photo on the billboard in Paris, that pathetic excuse for a man at the London studio drooling over her, every man's eyes devouring her tonight. This moment ought to have felt like the culmination of his elaborate revenge, the satisfaction of knowing that, contrary to what she protested, she wanted him. But it didn't feel like his desire was about anything else at all any more except the uncontainable need to bury himself deep within her—now. It had no interest in the past or who they were, and certainly no interest in tomorrow. It just *was*.

Moving, he reached behind her and clasped his hands around her wrists—impatient with her fumbling—and guided them to her sides. Pulling her towards him, he placed his fingers at the dip of her waist and traced her perfect silhouette upwards, stopping tormentingly short of the underside of her full, swollen breasts. *His*, he thought, dropping his lips to taste the skin below the sapphires, feeling her buck in pleasure.

'You like that, yes?'

She could hear from his voice that he was smiling as he dipped his head, his mouth caressing her neck, sending shockwaves of pleasure around her body.

'Mmm.' Even better she liked imagining just where he might trail his hands and his lips next, she thought brazenly, too consumed with need for her brain to alight upon a more coherent response.

But she wanted to look at him, to have his gilded expression alight on hers, to see the desire in his eyes once more. Clasping his head in her hands, she ran her fingers through the luxuriousness of his thick dark hair, directing him upwards, kissing him full on the lips, a kiss that told him she was his. However much she loathed the notion of belonging to anyone. If this was goodbye she needed to savour every second. Like a camel storing water in the desert, she had been parched of him for seven years; this had to see her through eternity.

Whilst she was distracted, he freed the zip of her dress and let it fall to the floor, taking with it the thin string of underwear that the outfit had demanded, and stood back to observe her unashamedly. She felt absurdly coy, stark naked before him except for the sapphires. Which in theory was ridiculous, because her job was inviting people to look at her—albeit not *quite* so intimately—but no one had ever looked at her like he did. She remembered with a start that it was the exact same self-assured, all-consuming appraisal he had bestowed upon her the day he had walked into the Jezebel photo shoot. At a distance, it had felt like being hit by an invisible bolt of lightning. Up close, it was like flying too close to the sun.

He strode forward, snaking one hand possessively across her waist and the other beneath her bottom, lifting her into his arms as he had done when they had stepped off his private jet. But here were no waiting paparazzi. Just a master bedroom festooned in enchanting reddish-purple. He strode through the doorway she had barely registered before and slowly lowered her down onto the bed.

She knew what was coming. But wasn't she supposed to be nervous about this moment? Nothing. Only the overwhelming desire to have him naked with her. She rolled over and kneeled up on the low bed, tugging at the luxurious dark

blue fabric of his robe, not knowing where to start and all the
more excited by the mystery.

He placed his hands on top of hers and guided them eroti-
cally, making it look easy. She told herself to commit the spe-
cifics to memory, then not to be so stupid for she would never
need to know again. Until his robe dropped to the floor and
the sight of his body prevented her from thinking any articu-
late thought whatsoever.

He was beautiful.

Tentatively, she reached out one hand to run her fingers
over the dark whorls of hair smattering his broad, hard chest.
He threw back his head in abandon, such an image of surrendered control that waves of delight flooded through her. His
muscles were hard, the veins in his arms looked virile…ready.
She dropped her eyes.

He was magnificent. Not that she was surprised, but the unashamed jut of his arousal fascinated her in a way she had not
anticipated. She wanted to touch it, stroke it, caress it. But,
just as she began to slowly brush her hand forward along his
thigh, he caught hold of her wrist.

'If you're not careful, *kalilha*, our moment will be over
before it has begun', he whispered, his voice like silk as he
slipped on top of her and finally cupped one breast so expertly
that she arched her back and stifled a cry of his name as his
tongue flicked across its peak, caught between the eroticism
of watching him and the need to close her eyes tightly in
order to ride the sensation.

Her eyes darkened in pleasure. Then, just as she felt she
might explode from the tantalising pleasure of it all, he slipped
his hand lower, meeting her warmth.

'Kaliq!' If she had imagined she was close to some kind
of crescendo, now she learned that she had only just stepped

on the first rung of the ladder, for the rhythmic touch at the innermost part of her sent her to some skyward world from which she never wanted to descend. And yet she wanted more.

'Make love to me, Kaliq.'

The second the sentence was out of her mouth her eyes flew open, her inexperience suddenly making her doubt the propriety of the statement, but he had already moved on top of her in answer, his knee parting her thighs, deliciously and hypnotically slowly. She had a vague notion of him slipping on a condom—protecting the royal seed, she thought ruefully—but the moment was still better than the best feeling she'd ever known.

'Please!'

He growled in satisfaction and, in one magnificent stroke, he was inside her. There was only one moment of acute resistance: his length was too hard, her own body too ready for him. But the look on his face as he froze above her was more painful.

He knew.

Of course he would; he was an experienced lover and she wouldn't have expected otherwise, *if* she had given that element of this particular moment any forethought, which she hadn't. For one hideous second she felt sure that he was going to withdraw, that he had no desire to make love to an inexperienced virgin. But, as she held onto her breath like a balloon she daren't release, her eyes searching his face, she saw that what was written there was not disgust but something else. Disbelief. The realisation that, for once in his life, he had been wrong. And then, as she wriggled her bottom, taking him deeper inside her, the question in his eyes was replaced with the flaring of unequivocal hunger and he began to match her movement, rocking slowly backwards and forwards.

His eyes never left hers. It felt even more intimate than the actions of their bodies, like the very first moment he had looked at her and something indescribable had passed between them. It seemed to rise out of the past and spill into the present, binding them inseparably. Tamara thought she would die from the sensation. It felt as if everything she had experienced in her lifetime up until this moment had been through the lens of a camera and now she was being given the whole picture in all its real life Technicolor glory. He moved so steadily inside her, with such unashamed and unabashed pleasure, that seeing the expression on his face alone had her moving nearer and nearer to the edge, as if she were now at the top rung of a ladder and there could be nothing greater than toppling over.

Whispering native caresses under his breath as her nipples grazed his chest, she could hear short, raspy, hell, *sexy* breaths issuing forth from her own mouth in a voice she barely recognised as her own. Growing faster, shallower. Then, as his hand reached down to mould her even more perfectly to him, it happened. The pulse in every one of her muscles quickened and tipped her over the edge. On the other side was an exquisite stillness which flooded her body and seemed to reach into her soul. She was only called back by the primal sound of Kaliq reaching his own peak as he rode home his final thrust, calling out her name.

CHAPTER NINE

KALIQ watched from beneath heavy-lidded eyes as Tamara padded around the nuptial chamber in nothing but a white cotton towel, examining their clothes on the floor like a nurse attending wounded soldiers after a battle. Apparently she was looking for something to wear.

She needn't bother.

He supposed she thought he was asleep, but he had stirred the instant she had risen from the bed and found her way to the bathroom, just opening his eyes wide enough to see her tantalising bottom disappear behind the door and feel the kick of his morning arousal. It surprised him. After sex, a woman's appeal usually diminished. Usually.

He wondered if she would blush if he reached out his arm and pulled her to him now, revealing that he had been watching her all this time. Until she began folding up last night's gown and he was reminded of when she had done something similar in her dressing room in London—men coming and going as if it were a thoroughfare—and knew she wouldn't bat an eyelid. Walking around virtually naked was part of her job.

So how the hell was it that she'd been a *virgin*?

He bit down on his lower lip as she bent down, the towel

skimming her thighs. He had never made love to an innocent woman before. Discovering that *she* was pure had shocked him to the core. Shocked him, and then filled him with a hunger unlike any he had never known. It made everything… complicated, and he prided himself on keeping his affairs with women unreservedly straightforward. In taking her he felt as if he had broken the ancient moral code he abided by, had done her the wrong he had taken pains to avoid seven years ago. Had she done that on purpose?

'You didn't think it prudent to tell me?'

His voice cut across the stillness of the morning and Tamara froze. She had been grateful to wake up and find that he was still asleep, to slip out from beneath the arm which had held her close in the night, to avoid the inevitable questions of morning. Like where she went from here, because the obvious answer was *home*, but it felt like home was in his arms.

'Tell you what—that I wished to take a shower?' she asked, playing for time, ignoring the faint ache between her legs and trying not to think about how much she longed for him again. 'I'm sorry, you seemed so fast asleep.'

'I wasn't talking about the shower.' Although now he was thinking about it—the warm water running over those breasts and her beautifully flat stomach, caressing the legs she had knotted behind his back as he had taken her.

'No?' She queried as casually as she could muster, tidying her hair in the mirror.

'You didn't think it prudent to tell me that you are—' he blinked like a sceptic observing a magic trick '—that you *were* innocent. That you had never known a man in that way.'

Tamara brushed the long layers of her fringe to one side, not really seeing her own reflection.

'I didn't think it was important.'

'Important?' It was almost a roar and he sat up instantly, the sheet falling away. The sight of his spectacular tanned body in the light of day was dangerously distracting. 'Virginity might count for nothing in your society, *kalilha*, but in Qwasir we consider it a gift when a woman chooses…to give herself to a man for the first time.' Despite his remonstrations, the underlying satisfaction in his voice was undeniable.

'Well, then, I'll consider myself excused from sending you a birthday present next year then, shall I?' she said sarcastically.

Kaliq felt his blood run cold. A more devious woman might have lured him into taking her virtue in order to prompt a proposal of marriage. Not Tamara. That thought was clearly just as repellent to her now as it had been then, not that he had any intention of putting his pride on the line a second time, no matter what propriety demanded. He frowned, a new feeling inside him opening up, as if someone had gashed his flesh open from the inside out.

'You deny that it is of any consequence that you chose to give yourself to me?'

She tried to keep her voice steady; she was hardly going to admit that since his proposal she had been too afraid that every man had a hidden agenda to risk such intimacy. Or inflate his epic ego by admitting that she had never wanted anyone else like she wanted him anyway. 'All creatures have carnal desires, do they not, Kaliq? I'll admit I wanted you, as you wanted me. But I can assure you there is nothing sentimental about the fact that you were my first.'

She said it as if he was just one in a long line and had happened to find himself at the front of the queue. He had never met a woman so lacking in feeling! Or a woman so responsive in his arms, he groaned inwardly, knowing such fire and ice was a deadly combination.

'Do not tell me then that your carnal desire is satisfied after only one night, *kalilah*.' His voice was silky smooth as he moved towards her.

'My contract here is over.'

'What if I wish you to extend it?'

Perhaps he ought to have known better than to give the idea that suddenly came into his mind even a moment's consideration. But he dismissed his doubts by telling himself it was just an extension of what he had been planning all along, too relieved to have alighted upon a plan which would slake his desire.

'I have worn the jewels, Kaliq. Your trick for distracting the press has come to an end.'

'Or perhaps it is just the beginning.' He slid his hand across her back. She could feel the heat of his fingers through the towel and the press of his erection against her tummy. 'Don't you think that by now the papers will be filled with speculation as to why we rode off into the night together, you wearing the royal gems, when the royal gala was still in full swing?'

'Because I was in danger!'

'In danger of being leered at by every man in the room if we stayed,' he ground out. 'Jalaal informed me yesterday that since the minute we stepped off my private jet the papers have been rife with speculation that I am to announce you as my future bride.'

Kaliq saw a look of horror cross her face and gritted his teeth, telling himself that her coolness was the exact requirement for what he had in mind. 'That you are entirely unsuitable for the position will fill all the more column inches and leave less room for speculation about my father's health. Since neither of us have had our fill of one another and I have royal business on the island of Montéz, it is the perfect solution. You will accompany me there. As my fiancée.'

What? Tamara took a step back from the deceptively close proximity of his body and forbade her heart to soar. Nothing, that was what. He wished her to *pose* as his bride-to-be, as an extension of her modelling contract. For the good of his country and his libido, nothing else. And yet he *was* asking her to stay.

'Until you choose a bride for real?' she choked.

He frowned and paused for a moment, as if he hadn't thought that far ahead. 'Exactly. My royal duties have given me little time for such a task.'

'And what of your father—surely he wouldn't condone lying to your people?'

'My father has entrusted me to do the right thing for our country.'

'But you *would* tell him.'

'Several years after my mother died he admitted to me that he had once been so overcome with grief he almost abdicated.' Tamara's heart ached when she thought of the love his parents had shared. 'He made the right decision to tell no one at the time.'

'So no one would know but us,' she said to herself, knowing she would never wish to cause Rashid further pain.

Kaliq pulled her to him, his warm breath on her neck, the distinctive musky scent of him filling her nostrils, sending her hormones haywire. Was that the only reason she was considering this? It would be doing everything she loathed: living a lie, playing to the press and setting her heart up to be broken. But the press had already printed the lies. And she wanted to make love to him again more than anything else in the world.

Maybe, just maybe, this would get him out of her system for good. Making love to him had been more tender than she could possibly have imagined, but wouldn't playing his fiancée on some royal excursion prove once and for all that she was second to his duty? If she left now, she was in danger of telling herself the ridiculously high regard in which he held a woman's virginity was not barbaric chauvinism but admirable old-fashioned values. So long as Kaliq was in no danger of knowing she risked her heart, she was safe. She thought fast.

'I presume the financial rewards will be handsome?'

The second the words were out of her mouth, she remembered Mike and the Foundation, and was appalled that they had slipped her mind until now. But relieved. Because she told herself that justified everything.

Kaliq scowled and released her, refusing to allow himself to give in to the weakness of lust when she thought she could turn her desire on and off at a price. There would be plenty of time to prove he could make her beg for the pleasure.

'I will match the fee for last night. Per day. Good enough?' he growled, before striding off to douse himself in the cool stream of the shower.

Tamara sat on the edge of the bed, envisaging the droplets of water running in rivulets over the hard planes of his body, visions of last night rolling through her mind. Kaliq looking at her with those blazing dark brown eyes. The luxury of his name loud upon her lips, lying naked beside him, on top of him, beneath him. Imagining doing it all again. Her mouth went dry. Agreeing to his plan had been idiotic, but *not* taking the opportunity to make love to him again would have been worse.

Yet the minute he emerged from the bathroom she knew that they would lock the gems here and leave all this behind, return to the palace to prepare for their trip to Montéz. Her stomach was a mix of emotions. Apprehension. Excitement.

Most of all she was reluctant to leave the nuptial chamber, because last night it had felt like *their* little corner of the earth.

Or at least it seemed that way to her until they rode up to the palace on Amir an hour later, the bright sunlight glinting off its vast white domes, and she was reminded that Kaliq was not the kind of man who could ever be shut away in a little corner anywhere.

'I sent word of our return, and of our engagement,' Kaliq said as he helped her dismount, arrows of fresh arousal mixing with a sense of déjà vu. 'The King wishes to see you briefly, alone.'

'Alone?' Tamara gaped. She deeply respected King Rashid and had never been nervous about finding herself in his presence before, but surely this meant that either he was deeply unhappy about the sudden announcement of his son's betrothal, or he smelled a rat.

'He wishes to see me afterwards, but has requested your presence first. I'm sure it is nothing to warrant your concern.'

It was easy for him to say.

Tamara blushed as she was led into the royal dining room where she had met the King the other night. Where she and Kaliq had eaten dinner, had—

The door opened and the King entered. He looked healthier than when she had seen him last, the rosy glow returned to his cheeks, but at the same time somehow more fragile. She held out the chair for him and bowed respectfully.

'Thank you, my dear.'

A member of the palace staff came in with two glasses of elderflower water.

'Kaliq said you wished to see me, Your Highness?'

'Rashid, please.' He waved his hand. 'Indeed I do.'

He drew a slow breath. 'You looked enchanting last evening—from the photographs. And I hear you charmed the audience.' He smiled, looking into the distance. 'I was sorry I was not up to being there myself.'

Tamara instantly relaxed. 'Thank you. I think Kaliq would have succeeded in captivating them equally well without my help, but it was a privilege.'

The old man chuckled. 'I hear it is you who has captivated *him*, my dear. Congratulations.'

She nodded uncertainly as he reached out his hand to grip hers.

'I'm overjoyed. I was starting to fear I would never see the day.' He shook his head excitedly as if he was delighted that life could still deliver the unexpected, not seeming to notice the look of discomfort on her face.

He looked at her closely. 'I am sure your parents will be very proud too.'

'Perhaps.' She nodded resignedly but without bitterness, the kind of look that only came after years of disappointment.

'I met your mother once,' Rashid said frankly, 'when she and your father were very much in love. So much so, that he almost considered not accepting the post of ambassador for the time he knew it meant they would have to spend apart. But they were both so ambitious.'

Tamara did a double take, almost doubtful that she had heard the King correctly. She had never known her mother had met Rashid, even less supposed that her parents might have once been truly in love.

'After they divorced your father came to resent his job. It made him think of all he had sacrificed. It was a kind of grief, and grief affects us all in different ways.' His brow furrowed as if he had had a lifetime to contemplate it. 'I wonder if perhaps you remind them of mistakes they are too proud to admit they made too.'

Tamara struggled to remain composed. Had her parents apparent lack of concern for her all these years really been something else?

'Perhaps I have been a little short-sighted,' Tamara whispered.

'We are all that, my dear, until someone opens our eyes. As you have opened Kaliq's.'

Tamara looked puzzled.

'Contrary to recent interpretations, the whole purpose of the marriage clause in the Qwasirian law of inheritance is to ensure that the King remembers to be a *man*. Our forefathers knew that was essential in order to be a good ruler. Up until now, I think my son may have forgotten.'

Up until now? Tamara thought doubtfully. More like *forgotten, period*. If only Kaliq could be as emotionally astute as his father.

'And I was always so fearful of the opposite.' Rashid shook his head, staring out into the distance.

Her look of incomprehension remained.

'When Sofia…when Kaliq's mother passed away on the day of his birth, amidst my own grief I felt acutely the enormous responsibility that lay on my son's shoulders. Not only would he have to grow up with the weight of expectation which assails every crown prince, but the terrible burden of knowing that his mother's death was coupled with the beginning of his life. It was more than any child should have to bear. I thought that when he was old enough to understand he would rebel, turn his back on duty. I even prepared myself for it when he decided to study in Europe. But he did so in order that he might learn from the West, *exceed* the expectation on his shoulders. What I hadn't foreseen was that forgetting to find time for himself might be an equal cause for concern.'

Tamara stared at Rashid in disbelief for the second time in as many minutes. She had known that Sofia had passed away when Kaliq was very young, but not that it had been in childbirth. What would something like that do to a little boy, let alone a man? she wondered. All of a sudden she understood so much more. How he could be so forward-thinking and why he had chosen to study medicine in Paris, yet why his every action centred around his predestined duty. That duty was not only to honour his forebears, or for the good of Qwasir, but out of respect for his father, in memory of his mother. His mother, whose love he had grown up without. No wonder emotions didn't enter his relationships with women, that he was so closed off that he would fake their engagement for the good of others. And suddenly she couldn't lie to Rashid, who understood so much.

'Your Highness…this engagement. It's not what you think—'

Rashid held up his hand, silencing her. 'I think that for many years Qwasir has been waiting for my son to take a bride. He has never asked anyone, except you.' He shook his head as if that was all there was to be said on the matter. 'Do not forget that, whatever duty you happen to fulfil in the process.'

He rose abruptly and began to move slowly towards the door, before looking back with a smile.

'Enjoy Montéz. It was Sofia's favourite place. Outside Qwasir, of course.'

Tamara stared after him with affection, admiration and the sense that the fog of a lifetime had just cleared. She just didn't know what to think of the view.

CHAPTER TEN

IN THE last six months—since her modelling career began—
Tamara had been lucky enough to touch down at some of the
most picturesque places in the world. But the beauty of
coming in to land at Montéz was something else, second only
to the rousing landscape of Qwasir.

She could see the Côte d'Azure across the turquoise
expanse of the Mediterranean, all around her lush green hills
and nothing else for miles. Just a waiting sports car at the end
of the private runway, not a journalist in sight.

'So, *chérie*—' Kaliq grinned as he guided her to the
Maserati which looked suspiciously as if it had been custom-
painted A'zam blue '—welcome to Montéz.'

He slid into the seat beside her, the French endearment
doing things to her insides. She had forgotten how good he
looked in the driving seat—equally at home in black leather
or on horseback. Although she should probably be reminding
herself that neither his good mood nor what Rashid had said
meant this was anything other than royal business with a little
sex thrown in, not thinking about how remarkably good his
body looked anywhere. But after the glances he had been
giving her on the flight, so different from their last encounter
on his private jet, it was hardly surprising. There had even been

times when she had been convinced that he would dismiss his royal air stewardess and, though Tamara would have half-died with shame if he had, when he hadn't she had been tempted to tell her they needed no further assistance herself.

He twisted as he sat down, reaching inside the pocket of his chinos as if it held the keys to the ignition. But they were already in his other hand.

'Here,' he said casually, tossing her a small rosewood box, which she caught absent-mindedly before looking down and immediately lightening her touch. It looked centuries old, the design the same as the doors and dining table in the palace.

'What's this?' Tamara whispered, looking across at him as he started the engine.

Casually he checked his mirrors and pulled away. 'Something you're going to need. Don't tell me the thought hadn't crossed your mind.'

Tamara allowed his matter-of-fact tone and the careless way he had thrown the box to prevent her mind from reaching the obvious conclusion, but in her heart she had already guessed. She opened it quickly.

Then wished she had given herself time to prepare.

The ring was stunning. Stunning but simple. One single brilliant sapphire. It *was* a necessity for their arrangement, of course, but one that genuinely hadn't entered her head.

'I don't know what to say.'

'You're not required to say anything. Just wear it. We can have the size changed if it doesn't fit.'

Tentatively she placed it onto her finger, as if fearful that the minute she slipped it over her knuckle someone would strike her down. But no one did. And it fitted. Perfectly.

'It is something you already had?' she asked, fearful that her silence gave her away, needing to fill it.

'It was the betrothal ring my father gave my mother.' He took a bend at speed.

Sofia's ring?

'Sapphires were still being mined in Qwasir when my father was a young man,' he explained. 'That sapphire is by no means the most precious that was ever found—that award goes to the sapphires in the A'zam necklace, of course. But it was the last one.'

Tamara was silent. She stared at the ring in awe. The ring that was on the third finger of her left hand. He seemed to be concentrating on the road.

'You were hoping to select something new, stop off at Paris, perhaps?' he bit out.

'No, I just thought—' That if anything he would have hired an enormous flashy diamond, something utterly unsentimental?

'Thought what, Tamara?'

'I just hadn't considered I'd need to wear one.'

'It would look rather odd if you arrived to have dinner with Prince Leon without one, in light of the announcement,' he ground out. 'Betrothal rings—or engagement rings, however you choose to describe them—are an extremely important custom in Qwasir. We do not exchange wedding rings as in the West.'

Tamara looked faintly surprised. Come to think of it, she vaguely remembered reading that in her guidebook all those years ago, but the section on wedding traditions had held little interest for her.

'Why?'

'Because once a woman promises herself to a man it makes no difference whether they are married or not—she belongs to him,' Kaliq qualified, annoyed that she was questioning the ancient practice.

Tamara bristled. 'And once a woman is married, what need would she have of a symbol of the union as she goes about her own life, because she ceases to have one?'

'If you imply that after marriage she would always be by his side, then of course.'

'Which is why such a custom could never exist in the West.'

'Or perhaps Western women demand two rings because they are obsessed with material gifts,' he drawled.

As they soared along the low coast road, his foot on the accelerator, he wondered why he was letting her get to him. He knew she lived to flout the proper order of things, for monetary gain. Hell, she had even checked with him this morning that her payment for last night had already been transferred. But since discovering she was a virgin, it wasn't so black and white.

For seven years he'd believed she had turned him down because she couldn't bear a life in the limelight. Until he had seen that goddammed poster. *Then* he had been convinced it was because she had wanted her sexual freedom. And now? Now he was forced to question whether she simply hadn't wanted to marry *him*.

As crown prince, he rarely had cause to wonder what people thought of him. Fawning admirers came with the title, and though he tried his best to surround himself with genuine advisors, so long as they did their job well, their personal feelings were not his concern. So why did it frustrate the hell out of him that he seemed to be nothing more than a passing interest to her? He shook his head.

'So what royal business is it that you are here to conduct?' Tamara asked, sensing from the tension in his shoulders that she had made too big a deal of the ring. To him, it was clearly nothing more than a prop in their performance. She should have reacted with equal indifference; that it was Sofia's was only significant as part and parcel of the charade. It implied stability, the King's blessing. To the press. Not to her.

'Prince Leon wishes to discuss my recent international trading treaty and how it will strengthen the links between Montéz and the Middle East.' Kaliq frowned at his unguarded reply. The idea of a woman having any interest in affairs of state was new to him. No other woman with whom he had conducted a liaison had ever asked anything other than details about the luxuries of the palace, or why his time needed to be so consumed with business when he did not have to work to earn a living. But then he had never travelled on royal business with a woman before, no matter how much fodder he needed to give the press, nor how many times Leon had encouraged him to bring a female companion on his visits to Montéz. Until now, he had never allowed himself the distraction. He was beginning to see why. Because to hell with the treaty—all he was interested in was how soon he could take her to bed again.

He continued, 'The links between Montéz and Qwasir go back a long way. We began trading by water, and then by air. We are also great friends.'

The notion of Kaliq having friends seemed remote to Tamara. He meant politically speaking, she was sure. She wondered if she would find the sovereign prince as closed off as Kaliq.

'Will we meet the Prince this evening?'

'Indeed. After we have freshened up at my villa. At the time I thought it a wise idea,' he drawled, taking his eyes off the long sunlit road for a moment and drinking her in as if, given half a chance, he would reach for the handbrake, screech to a halt and lift her across and onto his lap there and then. But he didn't, and Tamara forced herself to look out at the beautiful view to concentrate her own wayward thoughts.

She had always wanted to visit the island of Montéz. Not just because her father had once written and told her of its beauty—the delightful coastline, majestic hills and intriguing city centre—but also because of its fascinating independence from the rest of France. Its school system was well-reputed throughout the world, and she had long hoped to have an excuse to visit as research for the Foundation, or for work. She'd never dreamed she'd be visiting as a guest of the Prince. That wasn't the sort of thing you could book as an optional excursion on a package tour, let alone schedule in as part of a gruelling Jezebel shoot.

She didn't know where to look first as he drove them along a narrow winding road up the mountainside and rolled the Maserati to a standstill before the low building which was painted the colour of ripe mango. Aleppo pine trees surrounded the crazy paving of a terrace area bedecked with white bistro-style table and chairs, a grass verge leading down to what sounded like a swimming pool and behind them a full-sized tennis court.

'It's beautiful!' Tamara gasped, throwing open the door of the car and jumping out. 'How did you find this place?'

Kaliq followed her. 'The friendship between my family and Leon's goes back generations. My father always made time for us to holiday on this island. We stayed at the palace but Leon and I would wander up into these hills. My father told me that my mother used to call it Le Jardin de la Mer. I had the villa built whilst I was studying in Paris as an escape from city life—' he shook his head '—but lately it seems to have turned into a base for business.'

The Garden of the Sea, Tamara translated, stepping forward to take in the incredible vista of acres of green, the bright blue sea and endless sky, deciding Sofia had been spot on. Then she turned back to survey the house, its stunning grounds, the incredible facilities. There was one in particular she was itching to try out.

'So, do you want to?' she asked mischievously, hands on hips, turning back to see Kaliq looking devastatingly sexy as he leaned against the car, the sunlight catching the tinted windscreen.

Kaliq raised the corner of his mouth into a suggestive smile. 'Want to what?'

'Play tennis, of course.'

'Tennis?' He couldn't recall ever having used the court, and it sure as hell wasn't on his mind at the moment.

'Why not? Didn't you say you built this place to relax in? Plus there's the perfect breeze and the glare of the sun is on the pool right now.' She raised her eyebrows in challenge. That, and a little physical exertion in the form of her favourite sport, might take her mind off the terrifying prospect of having to lie through her teeth to the Prince of Montéz about her relationship with Kaliq. 'We've got plenty of time before we have to go to the palace.'

Kaliq barely had time to respond in the affirmative before she was leaning inside the boot of the car, rooting around in her bag and producing a scrap of something white, which she pulled on under her summer dress.

Still leaning against the front of the car, he stood absolutely still, watching her through the back window, catching a glimpse of flesh as she discarded the dress and exchanged it for a white vest top. Slipping trainers onto her feet ought to have had the effect of making her look *un*adorned, but somehow only drew attention to the natural length and shapeliness of her long brown legs beneath the short flared skirt.

'It's not technically meant for sport—' she shrugged, following his assessing gaze '—but it'll do.'

Kaliq was well attuned to women's subtle hints for compliments or the promise of new clothes, but as he watched her standing there, so utterly ingenuous, he knew that she was asking nothing of the sort. In fact, she was asking nothing of him whatsoever and he wasn't used to that at all.

'Are you playing like that?' she asked, walking over to him in response to his silent stare, plucking at the corner of his shirt.

'You know if you wish for me to take off my clothes, you only have to ask, *oui*?' He unbuttoned it before she even had the time to consider that her words had been asking for trouble, leaving her to gaze open-mouthed at his aggressively healthy chest. The dark line of hair was all the more tempting now she knew exactly where it led.

'But, since you did not,' he said huskily, 'I believe I have something suitable in the car.'

Tamara sucked in a sudden breath as he brushed past her and moved to the back of the Maserati. The car was so low that if she had turned she would have seen everything, but she told herself it was one thing to agree to mutually pleasurable sex for the duration of their arrangement, another to be permanently leering any time he came near her without his shirt.

So she wandered off to the tennis court, daring herself not to look back, and almost succeeded. Until she entered the small summer house in which she found the rackets, a ball, and a window she could peer through without being seen.

He was ruthlessly competitive. She was glad, because so was she. When she played men at her local club they were always letting her win, fouling serves and falling over themselves to celebrate her points. It bored her to tears.

They must have been playing for at least forty-five minutes. When he had first emerged, wearing a tight T-shirt

and shorts, she had wondered how on earth she was even
going to keep a grip on her racket, but she had channelled her
frustration that she hadn't suggested they play something of
a different nature into the agility of the game, and now they
were neck and neck.

It was a new experience, seeing him like this. In fact, everything felt different since they'd arrived. As if they were any
other couple on their summer holiday. They weren't, of
course, she knew that, and yet here they were playing tennis
when she had felt sure he'd make an excuse—have some
papers to be going over or an important call to make before
this evening. The only time she had seen him loosen up previously was when he had shown her around Qwasir seven
years ago, but they'd never really been alone then, and she'd
later discovered he had been motivated by duty all along.
Now he genuinely seemed to be allowing himself to relax.

'Out!' she called as his return bounced down on the wrong
side of the line.

Kaliq watched her, her hair mussed from their energetic
game and clinging to the sides of her face, utterly oblivious
to just how sexy she looked.

'In,' he replied defiantly.

'That was nowhere near! You come over here and stand
where I'm standing—there's no way that was in.'

It was precisely the invitation he wanted. He cleared the
net easily.

'Perhaps if you show me exactly where you were standing.'

Tamara thought she was going to go up in flames as he came
up behind her, the back of his hand skimming her forearm.

'Maybe I *was* mistaken,' he breathed. 'Standing here,
things are a lot clearer.'

'Mmm.' Like the fact that when he was standing inches

away from her she could only think of *one* way to channel her desire.

'Out, then. Talking of which.' He lifted his arm to look at his watch.

Tamara's face fell. She had been so absorbed in him, in the game, she had forgotten they were supposed to be getting ready to go out. If they were to be on time, which of course they had to be, they would need to leave in fifteen minutes.

'Unless, of course—' Kaliq spun her round to face him '—we are too tired after the flight.' He raised his eyebrows provocatively.

'Kaliq!' Tamara exclaimed in surprise, delight and disbelief. 'You can't be suggesting we don't go?'

'Really, Tamara, I thought defying people's expectations was your favourite pastime.'

'We can't just turn down a royal invitation.'

'Oh, but you won't be, Tamara, you'll just be accepting a better one.'

CHAPTER ELEVEN

TAMARA didn't kid herself that if Kaliq's business with Leon had been urgent he still would have cancelled, but she couldn't help feeling astounded that he had postponed his royal duty to spend time with her.

Or grateful when he announced that dinner with the Prince was rescheduled for Tuesday.

'Three days from now?' she asked disbelievingly as he rejoined her on the terrace with a bottle of Pinot Noir and two towels. 'Did the Prince mind?'

Kaliq laughed. 'I think he was delighted to hear that even I am prone to the weaknesses of the flesh.'

'What?'

'Exhaustion, remember?'

'Oh,' Tamara breathed, biting her lip as she watched him set down the bottle of wine on one of the small tables and slowly begin to peel off his T-shirt, wrapping a towel around his neck.

She had resisted him shirtless once that day; to do so twice seemed an impossibility. Her pulse began to beat insistently in her ears, drowning out the early evening hum of cicadas. The tennis racket she had been using as a fan slid to the floor.

He had forgone their royal engagement to be here. The thought made her feel light-headed, emboldened.

Her voice was a whisper as she stood up. 'I do believe the only way to combat exhaustion is to go to bed.'

He did not hesitate, lifting her easily in his arms in the manner she was growing dangerously accustomed to, and carried her across the patio and over the threshold. Not of his royal palace, but of the home he had had crafted for pleasure. Twenty-four hours ago she could barely have believed this place existed. Everything about it thrilled her. Yet she could pay no attention to its interior as he carried her through the unpretentious rooms, because her eyes were fixed on him. Astonishing, magnificent him.

He set her down on the bedroom floor and kissed her slowly, thoroughly, as if they had a lifetime to savour each other. He reached his hand up her skirt, exploring, cupping her bottom. And then all of a sudden his thumbs slipped into her plain white briefs, removing them effortlessly, the rush of cool air and the heat of his hands making her bite her lip to stop herself crying out before they'd even begun.

But, rather than tossing her panties aside and returning to her heat, he examined them on the end of his finger, frowning.

'What?' she asked impatiently.

'You wear some of the world's most exclusive dresses and yet underneath you have this,' he questioned in disbelief, 'who is this…Marks and Spencer?' He sounded mystified by the words.

She stifled a giggle. 'Wearing designer clothes is my job, Kaliq, it is not who I am underneath. Sorry to disappoint you.'

He waved his hand aristocratically. 'You do *not* disappoint me.'

'Oh.' A thrill shot through her, stripping away any remaining fears about her inexperience. She slid down his body until she was kneeling on the floor, tugging at the waistband of his trousers.

'And you are one of the most powerful sheikhs in the world, from a stock of men who have survived the unrelenting conditions of the desert without aid for generations, and yet you feel the need to wear boxer shorts?' she retorted playfully.

He frowned haughtily, pushing off the offending underwear.

'Do not worry, Your Highness,' she said throatily, his manhood springing free, 'you do not disappoint me. But would you be disappointed in me if I did this?'

She trailed her lips over his belly, tasting the tip of his arousal.

'Oh, yes—I mean no!'

'You want me to stop?'

'No, please don't stop.'

And stop they didn't. They made love so many times she lost count. In the bedroom, in the shower, even once in the summer house after he had beaten her at tennis. Sometimes, it felt as if Kaliq were some sensual teacher introducing her to the exquisite art of lovemaking. Other times, he seemed to find her desire to satisfy him equally new, as if they were discovering mutual pleasure together.

She thought her inhibitions had been well and truly lowered in the heart of the desert, but she now understood that in the betrothal chamber she had been fettered by a constant awareness of what he was and what she wasn't. Now, in her mind's eye, they seemed anonymously suspended between East and West, as if balancing somewhere in the middle was actually a possibility.

For in the days that passed, they didn't just make love. They wandered down to the port together to buy fresh fish, to explore the lively market. She laughed at him as he pondered over the price of groceries, as if shopping was something he did every day. But here, Kaliq revealed, because of Montéz's strict laws against the press, he could do so in relative anonymity. She could comprehend then how it was that the same man who used the paparazzi for his own ends could have professed to hate their intrusion in the past, maybe still did. They talked about everything and nothing as they made dinner together, eating outside with the view of the royal palace on the opposite hill like a beautiful firefly in the night sky. Another bottle of wine left on the table half-drunk as they disappeared off to bed, too impatient to wait for darkness.

And now it was already Tuesday, Tamara thought pensively as she lay beneath the cool white sheet, listening to the sound of him breathing, feeling the early morning sunlight pouring through the thin gossamer curtains, his arm slung proprietorially across her waist. She decided it was the best way she had ever woken up. Particularly because the day ahead promised to deliver equal pleasure. Last night he had insisted that today they must take a boat across to the French coast and dock in the pretty harbour at Sainte-Maxime for lunch. Lunch, she thought. On his yacht in the middle of the Mediterranean. That wasn't about sex. Or the press. It was… What was it?

The muffled sound of a phone ringing interrupted her thoughts. She frowned, realising it was her mobile. For a moment she thought it might be her mother, her father even. No doubt news of her engagement would have hit the British press by now. She felt a pang of guilt that she hadn't told them herself. She swung her legs out of bed and tiptoed across the room to find her handbag, scrabbling through its pockets. The caller display allowed her to breathe a sigh of relief.

'Mike—hi!'

* * *

Kaliq had been dreaming. He couldn't remember the last time he had. In his dream he was a boy, running amongst the pines with Leon, playing some game where they defeated evil without anyone knowing who they really were. But then the dream morphed in the way dreams do, and it was Tamara amongst the trees and she was darting away from him, wearing the white skirt she had wriggled into to play tennis, his frustration building.

The sound of something ringing far away made him stir, but it was her voice that woke him. The sound of her voice saying another man's name.

He placed his hands on either side of his body and pushed himself upwards to see her walking out of earshot. Mike? Was that the pathetic excuse for a man he had had to liaise with at her cosmetics company? No, he had the same name as that corpulent British monarch. So who was Mike?

Not that it mattered. Jealousy was one of those emotions he didn't do, like regret. Because he had never needed to. Why would a woman even look at another man when she was with him? Especially one who had entrusted him with her virginity, however much she argued that that meant nothing.

Yet it irritated him that she slid open the glass door at the back of the bedroom to conduct her conversation. She must have sensed him wake, so why disappear? He hadn't, on the few occasions he'd chosen to take a call from Jalaal or his father. Which had, incidentally, been rare. Because from the moment they had played that spontaneous game of tennis he'd been reminded of why he had built this villa in the first place.

Kaliq watched her grimly as she twirled her dark auburn hair between her fingers, her voice just audible. Evidently, *work* was still uppermost in her mind.

'The money's cleared already? Excellent, I'm working on getting more to you now.'

Kaliq fought the urge to go over there, fling the door wide open and toss the damned mobile over the edge of the mountain but he thought better of it; that was exactly what someone who was jealous might do.

'Yes, he's set it all up, no—so that plan won't be necessary. There'll be more to spend elsewhere.' Tamara took a step further away then, her voice lost on the air.

Anger gnawed at him. She had made it clear when she'd accepted this arrangement that it was about the money, so it oughtn't have bothered him. But in the last few days she had *seemed* to care so little about material things. He shouldn't be surprised; she was always saying one thing and then doing another. Pretending to loathe the prospect of being in the public eye, then taking a job as a model. Playing the temptress, who was a virgin all along. There *could* be any number of principled reasons why she was giving his money to a man named Mike. But it didn't change the fact that she was hiding the truth. Well, he thought, now was her chance to reveal it.

Tamara crept back into the large master bedroom to find Kaliq sitting up in bed. It was an image that never failed to make her heart turn over, and it did now, though his features were clouded with an expression she couldn't fathom.

'I was awake; you needn't have gone outside.'

She replaced her mobile in her handbag, avoiding his gaze. She had sent Mike a text a couple of days ago to inform him that the funds were on their way, and to let him know that he need no longer be concerned about the school situation in Lan. He'd just called to discuss the details, but to have done so in front of Kaliq would have meant an explanation she couldn't face.

'Someone calling to congratulate you?'

She paused. 'Yes, a friend.'

'Tell me about him.'

The question startled her.

'Sorry?'

'Mike—is that his name? You asked me all about Leon.
Don't you think before we join him for dinner this evening I
should know these kind of details?'

It would have been the perfect time to reveal all of it. But
the thought of even trying felt as if she would be shedding
a layer of skin before she was ready. It would leave her too
raw, too vulnerable. For many reasons. There were the usual
ones, such as the fear that he wouldn't believe her, that it
would sound like a publicity stunt, but then there were a
whole host of others. If he asked her why, she'd have to
admit that it had only been when he had shown her that
school in Taqwasir that she had pushed aside her bitterness
at her own childhood and realised how lucky she had been.
And that would reveal that he had opened her heart all those
years ago, would make it obvious that she wasn't here
because she wanted the money, but because she wanted him.
It was far, far too dangerous.

'Like I said, he's just a friend—from work. Keeping me up-
to-date on the progress of things. There's not much to tell.'

She was being evasive. It infuriated him. Cool. Detached.
The very reasons why she was the perfect choice to pose as
his fiancée. But it got to him. He wanted her to admit she was
here because she couldn't get enough of him and because
she'd lost all desire to return to her life in London, to admit
that this was the path she should always have taken. Instead,
it was all about money and he didn't even know why. Well,
he'd make damned sure he found out, whether she was
prepared to tell him or not.

'And how *are* things progressing, Tamara? What with your

earnings this week, you must be pretty solvent. You never mentioned what you planned to do with them.'

She pulled on her cotton kimono and wrapped it around her body. 'I haven't decided yet. Perhaps I shall treat myself to some designer underwear.' She half-laughed, trying to draw the conversation into easier terrain. 'How are the shops in Sainte-Maxime?'

He clenched his teeth. 'I have some business I must conduct at the embassy today.'

He had given her the chance to be honest and she had failed. Well, there was no way he was going to spend the day paying her to *act* as if she was enjoying herself. He'd find out the truth by his own means.

'I will be home before Leon's chauffeur arrives to collect us.'

She nodded slowly. 'Of course.'

It was funny how, once she was alone at Le Jardin, all the things she loved so much about it became all the things she couldn't face. The sprawling open spaces which had appeared to be a boundless paradise now felt solitary. The tennis court looked redundant and the beautiful French-style kitchen with its generously loaded pantry seemed gratuitous. She wouldn't have bothered with lunch at all if she hadn't remembered that tonight she had a duty to perform, and it would be no good being so light headed after one aperitif on an empty stomach that she couldn't stand up straight. Not that she approved of skipping meals, she had a healthy appetite, but today she was hard pushed to find it.

By the afternoon, though, she had almost convinced herself that her disappointment was a good thing and had taken herself off into the nearest town to see if she could learn anything about methods of schooling from the new university of Montéz. After all, being pushed aside for his duty was exactly what she had supposed this trip would entail, what she *wanted* it to entail. To reaffirm that, had this been real, she never could have borne his lifestyle. She had just been weakened by that conversation with Rashid, and hadn't expected the last three days to have been the best in all her twenty-six years.

But though she should have known his tenderness couldn't last, his actions that morning were still puzzling her by the time evening arrived and she found herself standing before the contents of her wardrobe. Perhaps he had simply decided that three days holed up with her was long enough for the press to draw all the conclusions he required. But he had seemed annoyed too. Was it her mention of work? She knew her modelling was still repellent to him, no matter how convenient it had been to him this past week. She supposed she would never know, and that she ought to take that as reason enough in itself that theirs was the kind of affair that barely cut it as a holiday romance, let alone anything more.

Which was why right now she had to focus instead on the extra money this meant for another new school and how relieved she would feel when it was over, knowing how unsuited she was to being a prospective royal bride. But between now and then she still had to convince the sovereign of Montéz that she was Kaliq's fiancée for real. Gratefully, she lifted out the one evening dress she'd brought from England. Experience had taught her it was wise to carry one on shoots in case she was required to attend a function at short notice. It seemed an age ago that she had laid it in her suitcase, selected for a different purpose entirely, but, thankfully, exactly the one she would have chosen for this occasion too.

It was a dress that had been designed by Lisa, which she

had worn to promote her first fashion collection, the one that ended up kick-starting both their careers. It must have only been about half a year ago, but it felt like a lifetime for all that had happened since. It was a stunning shade of coral, strapless and long to the ground. Although Tamara appreciated the artistry of design, she was rarely overcome with the desire to own any particular accessory or item of clothing. But when she had put on this dress she had insisted that she buy it from Lisa there and then. It was made of chiffon and she had done something incredible with the ruching at the front which made it fall in delicate flutes to the floor. She had always felt as if it had been made for her. Funny, how it set off the betrothal ring on her finger to such great effect.

Tamara was just putting on a touch of mascara in the bathroom when she heard Kaliq return at six forty-four. She knew because she'd looked at the clock every thirty seconds for the last half an hour. Not in doubt that he would come— tonight was a royal duty, after all—but because, against her better judgement, she longed to see him again. The sight of him buttoning up the shirt of his tux over the bronze flesh she had tasted with her tongue less than twenty-four hours before reminded her why.

'Did you have a productive day?' she asked levelly, determined not to let her disappointment that they had not spent it together enter her voice.

Kaliq almost laughed. It had been the most unproductive day he could ever recall having, and he loathed wasting time. He had briefly called Jalaal and asked him to investigate who 'Mike' was by putting a trace on the money transfers, but that would take days, maybe weeks. He had then planned to discuss new policies with his team at the embassy and investigate the efficiency of the current consular service, but somehow had ended up staring out of the window at the ocean, wondering why the hell he wasn't making love to Tamara on his yacht.

'If I answer yes, do you hope to persuade me to postpone dinner a second time?'

'No. I…I'm ready to go.'

'Oh, I can see you are perfectly *ready to go*, Tamara,' he said slowly, reading the desire on her face, his eyes dropping to what looked to be a wildly expensive dress. What had ever possessed him to believe she wasn't the materialistic *jezebel* he knew she was?

'You don't like it.'

'That is not what I said. I would rather see it safely back in the wardrobe and you wearing nothing at all.'

'Well, that would be an unforgettable look.'

'I thought *unforgettable* was what you were going for?'

She blushed. 'No, I was going for royal bride-to-be.'

'Really?' he said slowly, looking at her intently.

Tamara broke his gaze. 'Well, that is what you're paying me for.'

Kaliq's mouth tightened. 'How could I forget?'

CHAPTER TWELVE

THE French palace was as beautiful up close as it had looked from Le Jardin each evening at dusk. But though the air tonight was as warm, and Kaliq's presence at her side just as intoxicating, it could not have felt any more different. Because they were no longer simply two lovers losing track of time in their own little world; he had made that abundantly clear this morning. No, he was Prince Al-Zahir A'zam, whose every second was utilised in his duty to Qwasir. And she…she was a fool. For allowing herself to believe that he could ever have been anything else.

'Perfect timing,' he said with satisfaction, looking sharply at his watch as they reached the grand archway which formed the entrance to the royal palace, inadvertently proving her point. The guard nodded in recognition and directed them up a sweeping outdoor staircase with a red carpet running through the centre. Tamara was just about to ask whether they had to take it up every time it rained when a formidably handsome Frenchman wearing a navy jacket with gold braid approached them and she thought better of it.

'Kaliq! It has been too long.' The man embraced him affectionately. 'I should not have forgiven you had you not come in the wake of such great news.'

'Leon, it is good to see you.' Kaliq took a step back. 'May I introduce my fiancée, Miss Tamara Weston.'

The Prince surveyed her appreciatively before extending his hand. 'I am delighted to meet you, Miss Weston. Please accept my congratulations.'

'Merci, c'est un plaisir pour vous rencontrer aussi, altesse.' She curtsied lightly.

'Your French is impeccable. I'm impressed.' Tamara saw Kaliq visibly flinch out of the corner of her eye. Leon continued, 'I have been telling Kaliq for years he must bring a guest to Montéz. I see now he was just waiting for someone who met his exacting criteria.'

'And in the meantime he thought he would bring me,' Tamara replied ironically, looking directly at Kaliq.

Leon laughed heartily as he led them up the stairs and through to the enormous eighteenth-century dining room. 'And now I am convinced you are also exactly what he needs, Miss Weston.'

Kaliq gritted his teeth, disturbed by his own wave of annoyance. 'Do not tell me *you* are unaccompanied this evening, Leon.'

Just as Leon was about to retort in kind, the answer walked through the door.

'Ah, Cally,' he said testily, 'you decided to join us.'

Tamara turned to see a beautiful redhead in an asymmetric jade-green dress enter the room and slant a look of displeasure at the French prince. Tamara warmed to her instantly and, when Leon made the necessary introductions, was delighted to discover that she and Cally shared not only the same nationality but a reassuring lack of royal blood.

'Do you live here on Montéz?' Tamara asked her curiously as they took their seats at the antique dining table.

'I am just working on the island at the moment—'

'Cally is living here at the palace,' Leon interrupted. 'One of her many talents is restoring fine art. She is working on some paintings I purchased in London.' Though, from the way he couldn't keep his eyes off her, Tamara understood intuitively that their involvement went a lot deeper than that.

'It sounds fascinating,' Tamara said genuinely. 'I'd love to see.'

'I'd be delighted to show you.' Cally smiled as waitresses arrived with an enormous platter of meats, cheeses, olives and fresh bread.

How was it that two men born with such similar responsibilities upon their shoulders could be so different? Tamara wondered. Leon, who had time to indulge his passion for the arts, whose relationship with Cally didn't need to be justified in regard to his royal duties, or to anyone, for that matter. And Kaliq, who gave neither time nor space in his heart to anything but his duty, who was only conducting a relationship with her because it suited his royal purpose.

'So Tamara, how have you been enjoying your stay in Montéz?' Leon asked.

Tamara drew in a deep breath, pushing her feelings aside. 'Very much, thank you. You have a beautiful island.'

'You have done much exploring? I thought perhaps Kaliq would finally take some time to rest after the royal gala. My apologies, incidentally, that I was unable to attend. We were in London at the time.'

'No matter.' Kaliq waved his hand as if that evening had ceased to be of any importance. 'We have been to the market and the harbour, but mainly we have been at Le Jardin.'

'Although today I visited the new university just east of the villa,' Tamara added casually. 'I was very impressed.'

Kaliq's eyes narrowed. It felt as if the sharpness of his gaze was physically pricking her skin. 'You did?'

What else did she get up to that she failed to mention? he wondered. More private phone calls and bank transfers?

'Yes, Kaliq. Since you were working today.'

Tamara thought she saw Leon give a wry smile as he topped up her glass with the champagne he had insisted upon to celebrate their news.

'You must be used to exploring different countries by yourself,' Cally commented.

'I don't get as much time as I would like to explore when I am on a shoot abroad, but no, I don't mind travelling alone.'

'It sounds very exciting.'

So why did the thought of going back to that life now fill her with despondency? And why, even though she had been convinced that she would loathe the ostentation of this evening and feel completely out of place, did she find she was enjoying the company, that if she closed her eyes they might have been four friends from any walk of life, sharing food and wine?

'It can be.' She hoped her voice was convincing.

'It can also be very dangerous,' Kaliq cut in.

'Rarely,' Tamara replied, shoving her fork in her mouth, 'but occasionally in countries less civilised than France.'

Kaliq's mouth formed a thin hard line. 'Naturally, once we are married Tamara will give up work, so it shall cease to become a concern.'

Tamara almost choked on an olive but, before she had time to argue—albeit only in principle—Leon jumped in.

'So have you set a date for the wedding?'

'We are still deciding. It will be at some point between my royal engagements,' Kaliq answered, tactfully side-stepping the question as the main course of duck arrived.

Of course it would, Tamara thought. Heaven forbid it should interfere with that. *If* this was real, which it wasn't.

'Your father must be delighted,' Leon ventured. 'How is he?'

Kaliq looked grave. 'Slightly better, thank you.'

Tamara was surprised to find that, whilst Kaliq did everything he could to keep his father's health out of the newspapers, his condition was something he obviously discussed openly with Leon. But then she hadn't expected them to bypass formal greetings for a brotherly embrace earlier in the evening either. Obviously, their friendship was a lot deeper than she had anticipated. Part of her was glad; after all, hadn't she been desperately seeking evidence that he had a heart? Whilst the other part felt devastated to discover that he did, but had no intention of revealing it to her.

As Tamara looked around the table she noticed that Cally looked equally lost in thought, and for a moment she wished they could be alone to discuss what it was to be the woman of a royal male. Until she remembered that their relationships were far from comparable. Because whatever simmering tension existed between Cally and Leon, it was obvious to her that they were in love with each other. And she'd bet that if they did choose to marry, Leon would never dream of fitting their wedding in between his other duties or making her give up her career.

But that's never going to be your worry, she reminded herself as she dug into the delicious crème brûlée placed in front of her, which suddenly tasted bittersweet. For didn't tonight simply prove right every instinct she'd ever had about what life would be like married to him? Yes, it did, but in her heart she wanted him to prove those instincts wrong. And, in so many unexpected ways, he had.

Because she had held a bunch of preconceived ideas about the kind of ruler he would be in the same way he had about her modelling, and they were wrong. He was a ruler worthy of deep respect. She had witnessed it first hand at the gala, and was even aware of it now as he discussed his trading treaty with Leon, which she found to be irritatingly progressive. That, and because she had never dreamed that the night in the cave and the heady days at Le Jardin could have been filled with so much affection. But neither of those things ought to have swayed her. For the first didn't take into account his narrow-mindedness when it came to *her*, and the second overlooked the age-old truth that women were prone to attributing emotions to sex that men simply didn't feel. The realisation annoyed her, and she remained uncharacteristically quiet for the rest of the meal until she realised she had consumed her entire pudding and the mouth-watering French coffee without saying a word.

'Thank you, Leon, that was delicious.'

'My pleasure. I hope you will persuade Kaliq not to leave it so long between visits in future.'

Tamara pasted on a smile.

Kaliq nodded. 'So long as you promise to visit Qwasir soon so we can return the hospitality.'

'What an excellent idea,' Leon said slowly, looking at Cally. 'Now, you must forgive us but I find that *I* am now somewhat exhausted.'

Cally frowned. 'I thought perhaps Prince A'zam and Tamara would like to see the paintings before they leave.'

Despite her own emotional fatigue, Tamara was just about to agree that she would love to, when Leon interjected.

'Well, that will be an additional incentive for you both to return.' His tone was clipped as he signalled for his driver to bring the car around.

Cally looked incensed, but both her and Leon's goodbyes

were filled with genuine affection, Kaliq and Leon embracing once more and Cally wishing her luck with the wedding plans, that by the time they were seated in the back of the vehicle Tamara felt even more downhearted.

'You were quiet this evening.' Kaliq's tone was loaded with reprimand. It made her heavy heart fill with anger.

'Oh, I'm sorry, I thought you wanted your fiancée to be seen and not heard.'

'Do you suppose I would have selected you if I did?' His tone was scathing but low, as if wary that the driver would overhear. It irritated her even more.

'You mean you wanted me to be myself? Why didn't you say? I would gladly have announced that hell would freeze over before I'd give up my career for marriage!' she spat out vehemently. 'Was an announcement that I am never to model again really necessary?'

'Why, were you hoping Leon might employ you next? As a real life nude for his art gallery, perhaps?' he mocked.

'No, I thought, since none of this is real, you might actually be capable of *pretending* that you weren't a relic from the Dark Ages.'

Kaliq's nostrils flared and he shed his jacket. 'And do you think they would have believed that I would allow the future queen of Qwasir to continue as a cover-girl in between royal functions? It would be utterly inappropriate and entirely dangerous.'

'But you suppose they *were* convinced by my dutiful compliance?'

'I suspect they were too busy wondering why you went wandering off this afternoon without mentioning it to me.'

'You didn't ask,' Tamara said automatically, wondering how it was relevant.

'And what answer would you have given me if I had, I wonder? Would you have plucked one out of thin air, perhaps?'

Tamara folded her arms across her body and looked out at the night sky—cloudy, for the first time in days—as they ascended the narrow road to Le Jardin. 'I don't know what you're talking about.'

'Of course not,' he bit out sarcastically. As the car came to a standstill he flung open the door in frustration, Tamara following closely behind.

'If it hadn't been for your pressing royal business I would have been with you all day.'

He turned suddenly, his shoulders taut, rooted to the spot so firmly that, in her haste to follow, Tamara careened straight into his broad chest. Her hands gripped onto the muscles of his arms through the cotton of his shirt, the potent scent of his body filling her nostrils, the tiny distance between their bodies excruciating.

'Your Highness.' The male voice broke through the darkness and they split apart, turning to see Leon's driver stepping out of the car, anxiously holding out Kaliq's jacket, which in the heat of the moment he had left behind.

'*Je suis désolé.* I am sorry to interrupt, but your mobile phone is ringing.'

Her irritation that he answered it lasted only a second. Because, the instant he held the receiver to his ear, a look befell his face that she had never seen before.

Utter powerlessness.

And, even before he said the words, she knew.

For a second he took a step towards the hillside, looking out into the darkness of the night. Then, just as quickly, he turned round to face her, that expression shut away.

'I must return to Qwasir immediately. The King has

suffered a fatal heart attack.' *The King*, she noticed. Once she had thought such an address was unfeeling; now she understood it was simply the way he protected his heart.

'I'm sorry.' She hated the inadequacy of her words, but knew no others. Instead, she wanted to go to him, to hold the man she loved in his time of grief. Mourn with him for the loss of his father and a truly great man. But something prevented her. Because with the tragic loss of Rashid went her reason for being here. With no illness to distract from, no fake engagement was required. In order to inherit, Kaliq must marry for real: choose a suitable bride, and fast.

I must return to Qwasir immediately, she realised as he barked orders into his cellphone, not *we*. She nodded to herself, wanting to cry but knowing—however much it pained her—that tears were the last thing he needed tonight.

'Go,' she whispered, 'I can catch a flight back to London tomorrow.'

He looked at her, disgusted. 'Of course. *You* must be delighted that you can return to your career, I had forgotten.'

Tamara felt as if all the air in her lungs had been squeezed out, like a pair of bellows, and had lodged itself at the back of her throat.

'There is no joy in my heart tonight, Kaliq. Tell me what you wish me to do and I will do it.'

Her words offered to relinquish the independence she had spent her whole life fighting for, but she meant them with every fibre of her being.

'Be free, Tamara. Isn't that what you have always wanted?'

Yes ought to have been the answer. But it wasn't the one in her heart. Tamara shook her head, feeling all the weight of the night on her shoulders. What could she say—that she would gladly stay with him? And what would he do—extend her contract whilst he looked around for someone more suitable to supplant her?

'Kaliq…not to end this now would be…to mislead your people.'

Kaliq laughed a horrible bitter laugh that cut her deep. 'Now you pretend to worry about my people, *kalilah*? Go back to London, continue with your notorious career. Here—' he signalled towards the car '—Boyet will drive you to the airport, and I will arrange for the payment you are owed to be waiting for you when you return. What could be better?'

Tamara felt hot tears prick behind her eyes once more. But, before she knew what was happening, he had anchored his arm around her waist and had spun her round, so that she was crushed against his hard powerful chest as she had been only moments before. Only now his body was taut with grief and hers weak with regret.

His lips found hers with astounding speed and ferocity. It was the kind of primal, chauvinistic kiss that left her no choice in the matter, and if anyone had asked her she might have imagined it would be the best way to end this. Damning evidence of just how uncompromising he really was. But, in reality, it was the worst way of all. For as his hot, seeking tongue found hers—the kind of life-affirming kiss with such sheer physicality it could only come after an event which reminded a man of his own mortality—she saw with bright clarity that she belonged to him. That she always had and always would, whether that went against everything she professed to want or not.

His kiss lasted just long enough to tip her into the pitiful void of that realisation, but not so long that he was in danger of forgetting himself. He broke away from her and a sound, something like a storm filling the air somewhere above the grounds of the villa, roared loud in her ears. Disorientating and unfamiliar. But only to her.

'My helicopter,' he said in the same moment that she saw the alien-like craft dipping down towards the expanse of grass beyond the tennis court.

Suddenly, the wide abyss between her and his duty had never seemed so wide. Their separation never so final.

'Goodbye, Tamara.'

CHAPTER THIRTEEN

TAMARA stood in the grounds of Le Jardin like some Renaissance sculpture for what felt like an age after the sound of the helicopter taking off had faded away. Until finally, though the events of the evening were no more palatable, it occurred to her that it was the middle of the night and she was alone upon a French island where she no longer had any reason to be.

'Oh, Boyet, I am sorry!' she said, turning around to see Leon's driver still patiently waiting in the royal vehicle for further instructions. 'Give me two minutes to change and collect my things, if you *really* don't mind.'

She even felt ill at ease making use of royal transport now, but she could not bear to stay at the villa another night and, thankfully, the airport was on the way back to the palace anyway. Not that she knew the roads that well, she thought as they drove through the darkness, noting how unfamiliar they looked. Because, aside from that brief walk to the market and her own foray to the university that afternoon, she hadn't really seen that much of Montéz. But then—contrary to when she travelled for work and wished she could see more of a place than the location of the shoot and the four walls of her hotel room— all she had really wanted was to wake up next to Kaliq and have him to herself all day. The memories made her heart ache.

'*La radio, mademoiselle?*' Boyet asked softly.

'*Oui, s'il vous plaît.*'

Boyet tuned it methodically, stopping on the haunting melody of a piano. A deep male voice sang of love and loss and it seemed to reach into her soul and clasp it tightly. She closed her eyes and leaned her head back on the seat. She wanted to hold Kaliq. She should have held him. Not for her own sake, but because inside he was a boy who had lost his father and, though his country needed him to do his duty, she should have had the courage to tell him that as a human being there might be other things he needed too.

The song faded out and was replaced by a sombre-sounding French newsreader. She wasn't sure whether she was grateful that she could translate or not.

We are just receiving reports that Rashid Al-Zahir A'zam, the King of Qwasir has suffered a fatal heart attack. Although no official palace announcement was ever made about the King's declining health, there has been speculation about the likelihood of this event for some time. Concern now grows for the stability of the country, since King Rashid's only son Prince Kaliq must marry before he can legally inherit the throne. However, given the bachelor sheikh's recent engagement to British model Tamara Weston, the people of Qwasir must be hopeful that plans for the royal wedding are well underway. Without which, the country would surely face civil revolt.

Civil revolt? Tamara stared out into the blackness. Of course Kaliq had known his father was ill, as Rashid had done himself, but she had understood from the look on his face tonight that he had never imagined this would happen so soon. If he had, she felt sure he never would have gone ahead with this charade of an engagement. He had been using her to stem the tide of his peoples' fears until he could find a suitable royal bride, not to raise their hopes only to dash them when they needed hope most of all.

Though Qwasir was by no means a third-world country, the people looked to their ruler for strength and guidance. Their royal family were revered because they offered stability in a landscape consisting entirely of volatile desert. Without the guarantee of Kaliq to carry them forward, was civil revolt truly a possibility? It didn't bear thinking about.

Perhaps she shouldn't think about it, go back to London, having done what she'd come to do and resume her career. Except Qwasir concerned her, whether it ought to or not, and she had neither the desire to return to London nor felt she'd achieved her aim. Yes, she had modelled the gems, made the additional cash for the charity, but had she succeeded in getting Kaliq out of her system once and for all, had she convinced herself that she didn't want him? No, she couldn't have failed any more spectacularly at that.

Even her career had lost its appeal. Because, whatever high and mighty principles she had argued for in this car only an hour before, that kiss had confirmed that the only place she felt as if she truly had a purpose was with him. Regardless that he felt nothing for her.

That much had changed. Of course she wanted to hear that he loved her, as much now as seven years ago when she'd asked him why he was proposing. But she saw now that she would rather live without that than live without him altogether.

At least he had never pretended to have emotions he didn't feel. Now she was mature enough to be grateful for that. In the past she had thought him dishonest, acting as if he had a heart, then revealing it had been about his duty all along, but she had come to see those things simply coexisted within him. It was one of the reasons why she loved him.

As for marriage, well, her attitude to that had changed too. It was blinkered not to see beyond her parents' poor example. The reality was that you had to work at it, that some succeeded, others didn't. So what was the point of running away from the only man with whom she wanted to try and make it work, out of fear that it wouldn't? That was what she had done back then, in some desperate attempt to protect her heart. That was what she was doing now, driving through the streets of Montéz on the way back to her superficial life in London and further and further away from what felt like her destiny.

Destiny. It was an emotional, empirical term that Kaliq wouldn't approve of. But she'd spent years searching for hers and nothing but him had ever felt close. She could admit that now. After years of swearing to learn from her parents' mistakes, wasn't it about time she learned from her own? Didn't she owe it to herself to try, however remote the possibility?

'Boyet.' She tore her eyes away from the night and looked at his solemn face in the driver's mirror, suddenly sure of what she had to do.

'*Oui, Mademoiselle?*'

'Are there any direct flights to Qwasir from *l'aeroport*?'

If she had found it somewhat challenging to book a flight from Gatwick to Qwasir in the early hours of a Tuesday morning from the comfort of her flat, she suspected it would be even harder to find one from Montéz airport at midnight a week later, particularly as Boyet had shaken his head doubtfully at the chance of a direct flight.

When she reached the front of the queue for tickets, the pessimistic expression on the assistant's face seemed to confirm as much as she tapped away on her computer without looking up. Tamara felt her heart sink.

'You'll need to change at Paris, I'm afraid. The earliest available seat there looks to be at eight a.m., with a connecting flight at noon tomorrow.' She casually flicked open Tamara's passport, did a double take and looked up at her face in astonishment. 'But if you just take a seat in the executive lounge, Miss Weston, I'll see what my manager can do for you.'

If it had been any other occasion she would have insisted against preferential treatment, but the thought of having at least fifteen hours in which to talk herself out of this made her bite her tongue and, thankfully, the manager saw her onto a flight within an hour.

'Your fiancé will need you by his side, Miss Weston. Anything Med Airways can do to help.' He smiled.

Could you sky-write what I need say so that I don't have to? Tamara wanted to reply, but had thought better of any such gesture by the time the earlier plane he'd squeezed her onto had landed at Qwasir International after a few hours of broken sleep.

It was the first time she had arrived here without a royal-crested black vehicle waiting to escort her to the palace, and she could just imagine what Kaliq would say about her taking a taxi alone, but arriving unannounced would give her the advantage. That, and she was terrified that if she asked him to send a car he might refuse and tell her to get straight back on a plane out of here.

Thankfully, the taxi driver was kind-hearted, recognising her immediately and keen to converse in his broken English. If he wondered why she wasn't travelling in a royal vehicle he didn't say, for he was too absorbed in commiserating the recent and deep loss of the great Rashid and imagining the proud future that lay ahead under Kaliq's rule, once they were married. Tamara nodded and tried to smile, twisting the betrothal ring nervously around her finger.

It was nine in the morning when they drew up to the palace gates and she stepped out, her palms clammy as she handed over the fare, wondering if she wouldn't be wiser to stay in the car and tell the man to keep driving. Until she looked up and saw the crowds of women grieving and stopped thinking about herself altogether. Dressed in black, they had come together to celebrate a life and lament its passing. It was more vocal than her experience of mourning in the West, and extremely moving. Something Kaliq had said to Henry that day in the dressing room came back to her—that she had much to learn about the customs of his country. He had been right, she could admit that now. Could admit she wanted to learn about those customs too.

As she walked through the crowd the women stood back, bowing their heads in respect. But Tamara went to them, holding their hands, speaking the most reassuring words she could think of, whether or not they understood. And she saw in their eyes surprise at this gesture, which was customary to *her*. Saw their gladness, and their hope. For some inexplicable reason it fired her own.

The guard recognised her and opened the gate immediately. At least Kaliq had not left instructions that she was not to be granted entry, she thought. By the looks of it, he hadn't yet explained her absence either. Fully, at least.

'His Royal Highness is in the King's dining room, making the funeral arrangements,' the guard informed her discreetly as she passed him.

Walking through the white marble entrance, she was

suddenly nervous. She was tempted to kill time, to linger at the picture of Rashid and Sofia's wedding. But she knew that would only make her feel more sentimental than she dared allow herself to be. Either that, or it would make her lose her nerve.

Instead, she followed the guard's instructions, though what he had said only really sank in when she reached the rosewood door. *The King's dining room*, the one where they had so nearly made love—until he had spurned her. The one where King Rashid had welcomed her as his future daughter-in-law, had told her to remember she was the only woman Kaliq had ever asked. The room in which he was now making the arrangements for his father's funeral. She shook herself and knocked.

'Come in.'

His voice was terse. She knew her timing was terrible. But she couldn't imagine when a good time might ever present itself, and if she waited it would be too late. She felt the intricate wooden carvings of the door beneath her fingertips, drew in a deep breath and pushed.

If she had expected to walk straight in, look him in the eye and say it, she was going to be disappointed. She entered to see that he was neither alone nor paying any attention to who had walked in. His eyes were fixed on the crowd outside the window.

'Your Highness, Jalaal—' she bowed lightly, waiting for Kaliq to turn, but he didn't '—I apologise for interrupting. I just wished…I wished you to know that I am here and that, should you have a moment, I should very much like to speak with you.'

'So I gathered.'

'Sorry?'

'I have some phone calls to make,' Jalaal said diplomatically, picking up a bundle of papers from the table.

'Thank you,' Kaliq said to his aide, granting him permission to leave. At the sound of Jalaal shutting the door he turned sharply.

'I saw you arrive,' Kaliq said, inclining his head towards the window. 'Quite a performance. Unnecessary, under the circumstances.'

The sight of his face for the first time prevented her from any retort. He hadn't slept. She could see it by the five o'clock shadow at his jaw, the dark rings around his eyes.

'How the hell did you get here?'

There was no invitation to sit so she remained standing, her hands locked in front of her. 'I caught a plane to Paris and then a connecting flight.'

'And then what? You just paid anyone you could find at the airport to bring you here?'

'I took a taxi, yes.'

'After your last experience here, did it not occur to you that might be unwise?' He stood up, starting to pace.

'I am not wearing the sapphires today.'

His eyes dropped to her left hand, as if to check her statement, but the moment they both realised she was still wearing the betrothal ring was too awkward to acknowledge.

'You should have called ahead; I would have sent a car. In the eyes of my rivals—since they anticipate our imminent union—you are now more precious than any gemstone.'

She hadn't thought of that.

'You haven't told them yet.'

'I thought I would at least stagger the bad news over more than twenty-four hours.'

She nodded, understanding, grateful. 'The plans for the funeral are in place?'

'Yes, it is set for tomorrow, as is Qwasirian custom. And

yes, it is a public occasion, if you have returned in order that you might attend.' His tone was clipped.

She remembered what Kaliq had told her about his father almost abdicating after the death of Sofia. Having seen the crowd outside, she began to understand how difficult it must be to have something as private as grief become the property of the masses.

'I would be honoured to pay my respects. But that is not exactly why I have come.'

'Then why, *kalilah*—to collect the rest of your luggage?'

'I came because I heard something on the radio in Montéz that made me think.'

'And what could it have possibly been that would bring you back here, Tamara?' he said, growing impatient. 'A song perhaps. *The Show Must Go On? Money, Money Money*?'

In any other circumstance she would have laughed at a sheikh knowing the classics of Queen and Abba, but not today. She lowered her head.

'No, it was the news. Reiterating the law of inheritance. Expressing hope that the announcement of our engagement means plans for a royal wedding are already in progress.' She felt as if she were talking about another couple altogether, and she recognised in that instant that the two of them were entirely different people from the sheikh and the model the world believed they knew. She went on, 'They said that if it wasn't for our promised marriage then Qwasir might be facing civil revolt.'

A grave look furrowed Kaliq's dark brows. 'Go on.'

Part of her wanted to ask if it was true, but his expression told her asking wasn't necessary. 'I don't want that to happen. I love this country. I know I wasn't born here but every time I come back I feel like I belong.' She was babbling, she knew she was, but she needed to get it all out. 'But it's not just that. It got me thinking how we ended up pretending to be engaged in the first place. It wasn't just for the sake of Qwasir, it was also because…because the sex between us is fantastic.'

He stared at her, dumbfounded. 'You are telling me you have returned because you like my country and you want to have sex with me?'

She was getting hideously close to the emotionless list of reasons he had given her for his proposal in the desert seven years ago. But she had good reason. Keeping her feelings out of this was the only way she had any chance of convincing him that this was a good idea. Revealing that she had been in love with him for as long as she could remember could only hinder things unless he was in love with her, and he wasn't. So why risk a double-edged rejection?

'No, I'm saying that we both know if you don't marry soon it will be detrimental to Qwasir, and that—because of our own actions—your people already assume that you plan to marry me.' *Cut to the chase*, she told herself, knowing she was trying to avoid saying the words. Deciding there was a reason this had been left up to men since the beginning of time. Then convincing herself she'd never been one for convention anyway.

'Yes?' he said curtly.

'What I'm trying to say is that…under the circumstances… maybe the best solution might be to go ahead and marry me.'

He stared at her, his gilded eyes shuttered. Wondering if he had lost some of his razor-sharp ability to foresee what lay ahead because in the last twenty-four hours he had failed to see *two* things coming.

She was asking *him* to marry her.

It was the ultimate in female effrontery. Yet, somehow, coming from her it felt like capitulation. It irritated him that she was pretending that it had to do with his people, but he supposed it made no difference. What she was really admitting was that life as a royal was preferable to cheap celebrity, and whilst she had protested that her virginity counted for nothing, his bringing her to climax night after night had clearly counted for something.

So, finally—what was it the English said?—the boot was well and truly on the other foot. Nevertheless, he was surprised to find that he was *not* overwhelmed by the desire to say no. Instead, he felt the hard kick of arousal at the thought of finally possessing her once and for all. With no more lies, no more strutting around for anyone but him. To his surprise, alongside that desire came the realisation that it was also the most logical solution, though reason and lust for her had never gone hand in hand before. As she said, marriage as soon as possible was absolutely necessary for the future of Qwasir. *Absolutely necessary?* The thought suddenly made him recall that last conversation he had had with his father on the day he had announced their engagement—the one about re-inventing the wheel where matrimony was concerned. For a second it occurred to him that maybe he ought to check. But it only took one look into those bewitching eyes for him to dismiss it out of hand.

'You will give up your modelling career?'

Tamara felt arrows of disappointment shoot through her. Not because she had any intention of continuing with it, but because she had been desperately waiting for him to speak and she hadn't dreamed that his answer would hang upon some verbal pre-nuptial agreement.

'If I must.'

'Very well then.' He waved his hand and turned back to the window. 'That is settled. I shall see that we are married by this time next week.'

CHAPTER FOURTEEN

ONE week later, Tamara found herself staring at the oblong wooden box that Jalaal had just brought with as much disbelief as she had woken with each morning for the past seven days. Disbelief, and idiotic excitement. She had asked Kaliq to become her husband and he had said yes. Today she was going to marry him.

Tamara shook her head dazedly. If she had spent her life wanting to do something out of the ordinary, then she had certainly succeeded. Even if *he* had still managed to end up dominating *that* conversation—the one she sometimes wondered where she'd found the courage to even begin. Ever since, she had put it down to a night without sleep and momentary insanity. Not because of what she had asked, but that she had dared to ask it. Yet—however undeserving of her excitement his reasons were—he *had* said yes.

But whilst the way this wedding had come about might have broken the conventional Qwasirian order of things, in the formality filled days which had followed, he had made it clear that their marriage would not deviate from protocol in any other way. Except in one thing. Rather than a lavish public ceremony, he had insisted that this was to be an exceptionally private affair in the palace garden with only two witnesses—

Jalaal and Hana. No one else would know about their wedding until an announcement and a single photo was released to the press that afternoon.

When he had told her, though he had done so in the pragmatic tone he had used to notify her of all the arrangements, her heart had leapt. For a second she had allowed herself to believe that there was a dimension to this marriage which had nothing to do with stabilising the restless population and giving Kaliq his crown, but was just about the two of them. Until he had quashed that fantasy in the next breath.

'Are you satisfied?' he had questioned, as if consulting with his betrothed was a requirement written into some ancient decree, which he rather begrudged.

Tamara had nodded slowly, wary of revealing her delight.

'No doubt you would have preferred a star-studded event at the Plaza but, given that this is still very much a time of mourning, it is fitting that my father's funeral should be the public occasion and our marriage the private one.'

The reverse of every normal family ethic, she had thought amidst her disappointment, but aside from her hurt that there was not some more sentimental reason, it made perfect sense. It would hardly do for them to be all smiles for a thousand flashes only a week after the dignified funeral of King Rashid.

Tamara looked outside the window of the dressing room which, like the dining room below, faced the grand entrance of the palace. The funeral procession was gone now, but she could still remember every detail of that day. Standing with Kaliq beside the coffin, watching in admiration as he gave his eulogy. Of course he hadn't shown a flicker of emotion, solemnly playing the part that every camera of the world expected of him, and she had felt helpless. Until that night when he had buried himself in her body with all the life-at-testing physicality she had felt in his kiss the night they had first heard the news—the kiss that was so intense she had felt altered ever since. She told herself to take comfort in the knowledge that the incredible sex they shared was his release, the little piece of Montéz that they returned to each night. Sometimes, she thought it was her release too, but in a different way. Because it allowed her to express all the walled-up emotions she had to keep hidden during the day.

Today was no exception, for allowing herself to feel anything would only complicate matters, however much she couldn't stop remembering last night. As they had made love, he had looked at her with such intensity that she was dangerously close to wondering whether it *was* possible that once they were married he might open his heart to her after all. But she knew that was pure fantasy. Reprehensible too, because she'd promised herself that being his wife would be enough.

Telling herself to refrain from such futile thoughts, Tamara reached for the box. The sapphires. She had already guessed he would send them. It was what his birthright demanded, after all, and it was essential for her to be wearing them in the photo. Like the one of Rashid and Sofia. So why did holding them feel like her own personal fate? Because to him this might be a marriage of convenience, but Tamara knew she was only going to do this once. She took a deep breath, trying to contain her soaring heart as she walked towards the full-length mirror on the wall.

She had stood her ground on two things about this wedding. When she came to think of them now, they seemed silly womanly things. But they mattered to her. The first was her insistence that she dress alone. Kaliq had nodded as if he couldn't care a jot what she did before the ceremony so long as she turned up and signed the papers. Hana had looked offended, as if Tamara found her services lacking, but she had managed to pacify her by inventing special oils she might require for her pre-nuptial bath, and leaving her in charge of the wedding bouquet.

It was nothing to do with Hana lacking any skills. In truth, she was coming to think of her as a true friend, and she would have chosen her over any of the wardrobe or make-up girls from the Jezebel studio. But that was just it. She had spent the best part of a year being pampered and preened according to other people's tastes. To him, today might be an extension of that, but to her it wasn't about anyone but the two of them.

Which was why she had known she couldn't take her vows in anything other than one of Lisa's designs, especially since she was partly responsible for Kaliq crashing back into her life, albeit in a roundabout way. Tamara had called her mobile late one evening, with her fingers crossed that Lisa had something made up in her size that was suitable, given the time scale and that she was now one of the busiest designers in the business. But once Lisa had got over the shock that her closest friend was getting married to the Sheikh in just under a week, she had launched enthusiastically into a million questions about Tamara's ideal gown and insisted she put everything else on hold to make it right away.

Tamara didn't have one, of course—an image of *the dress* in her head. If she had done, she supposed she might have been the kind of woman who would have hurried down the aisle long before now. Nevertheless, as she stepped before the mirror in the gown that Lisa had couriered here yesterday, she saw that her friend had succeeded in creating something she might well have dreamed about if she had seen it before.

It was incredibly simple. A sheath dress of ivory organza and chiffon, with delicate sheer sleeves that gave a subtle nod to the demureness her position demanded. It somehow succeeded in blending elements from both East and West, which suited her perfectly. She placed the magnificent sapphires around her neck and waited for the feeling that this day ought to belong to someone else, but it didn't come.

There was a knock at the door. 'Miss Weston, I have your bouquet.'

'How many times do I have to tell you to call me Tamara?' she said softly as she opened it. 'Please.'

'Soon to be Queen Tamara.' Hana beamed as she handed her a beautifully simple spray of pale jasmine with a few blue delphiniums that mirrored the colour of the sapphires. She grinned at Hana's perceptiveness. Hana smiled back. 'Are you ready?'

As I'll ever be popped into her mind like a knee-jerk response. Except she realised with shocking clarity that it wasn't true. She nodded. She *was* ready—more ready than she had been for anything in her life.

Kaliq stood before the celebrant dressed in ivory robes embellished with gold, looking every inch like a king. It must have been the first time all week that he had actually stopped working. Even this morning he had been busy. Now that his wedding day was here, it had seemed fitting to get the preparations for his coronation underway, so he had gone down to the catacombs below the palace to unearth the ancient orders relating to the ceremony. He had handed them to his team on his way here. In theory, he could have left it to Jalaal to search the royal archive and begin the proceedings. If he was honest, he had been glad of the distraction.

Glad because it left him no time to consider what he had learned yesterday, when Jalaal had come to him with the news that he had finally discovered what Tamara had done with the money he had paid her. It had been so hard to trace because she had transferred it to a charity account called the Start-A-School Foundation. A charity which was run by a happily married man by the name of Mike Thompson, working on projects so close to those Kaliq was currently funding that he had asked Jalaal to double-check it wasn't some sort of bluff, but to no avail. All his digging had done was reaffirm his aide's findings, even discovering that she had visited the school in Lan without his knowledge. It explained everything—the phone call, her interest in the university in Montéz, everything except why hadn't she told him. So why hadn't he *asked* when he'd had the opportunity last night?

Because it suddenly seemed possible that she really was selfless enough to have proposed purely for the sake of Qwasir, a voice taunted him, and he didn't want to think about that. Or about how she had risked her life to protect the sapphires, comforted his people following his father's death, cared so little for ostentation all along. It had been easy when he could believe her motives were money and fame. And, though it ought to be irrelevant, it had been *preferable* to believe her proposal had at least something to do with *him*. Now it seemed possible that he was immaterial. Instead, she was taking on a burden of responsibility which, unlike him, she owed no one. It made him feel as if he was doing her a wrong, and yet—

'Your bride is here, Your Highness.'

Yet the prospect of having her as his wife—for the sake of Qwasir, of course—felt too much like an old itch finally being scratched to do anything but turn and watch her walk towards him.

He didn't know what he had expected. He had seen her

preened to perfection in high fashion concoctions, in make-shift tennis whites, in nothing at all. He had had no idea what she was planning when she had informed him she wished to use her own designer. It hadn't mattered so long as she was here, wearing the jewels, saying *I do*.

But he hadn't expected her to look…unmistakably natural, yet every bit a queen. Her dress unique but surprisingly traditional. The sapphires and the flowers bringing out the bright blue of her eyes. Effortlessly and undeniably beautiful. As she reached him he felt something indescribable open inside himself that he couldn't remember ever feeling before.

'Incomparable,' he whispered in her ear as she reached him.

Tamara decided it was her favourite word in the whole of the English language—of any language.

She hadn't been prepared for him to look at her that way as the ceremony began in the shade of the desert palm beneath the midday sun. That rather than just repeating a legal declaration, she would find herself fighting to swallow down the knot that rose in her throat as she promised to care for him always, blinking back the tears as he promised to do the same.

Most of all, she wasn't prepared for the feeling when the celebrant pronounced them husband and wife. It was a feeling she had been waiting for her whole life. The overwhelming certainty that there was nowhere else on earth she would rather be.

'*Bassam*—smile,' Jalaal said, standing before them both with the camera at that exact moment. But she already was.

He kissed her as Hana sprinkled petals over them both, and the four of them walked slowly back into the palace and through to a modest drawing room where lunch had been prepared. Kaliq squeezed her hand as he pulled back her chair.

'What are we having?' she asked, thinking that she'd better say something or she was in danger of telling him she loved him.

'A local dish,' he said, the corner of his wickedly tempting mouth lifting into a smile, 'made with chicken and quavas. I think you'll enjoy it.'

Tamara blushed in pleasure and remembrance.

'I am sure I will.' She nodded knowingly.

As they tucked into the delicious meal, she thought about tonight, when they would return to the nuptial cavern in the desert; about tomorrow, when they would begin the rest of their lives officially together, sleeping each night in the royal bedroom. The one whose location he had once said she would never need to know, yet somehow now she did.

'Your Highness, I mean Tamara,' Hana whispered, still overwhelmed by her participation in the day's events, but bolder thanks to a glass of champagne. 'Must I still be secret about your marriage?' She looked around the drawing room covertly as if it were full of dignitaries she simply couldn't see.

'No, Hana.' Tamara smiled, looking at Kaliq and then back at her. 'Kaliq has already prepared a statement explaining that we have married, and—' she looked further down the long table '—Jalaal has actually just gone to release it with a photograph now.'

Hana nodded excitedly, as if the whole of Qwasir sharing in their joy was the best thing she'd ever heard, as Jalaal re-entered the room just in time for dessert.

But he didn't join them immediately, hesitating at the door as if uncertain whether to bring with him the envelope in his hand or leave it outside the door.

'What is it?' Kaliq asked in the manner of someone who had received too much bad news of late to beat about the bush.

'Nothing serious, Your Highness.' He looked at Tamara, and then at the pavlova of a wedding cake that had been brought out in celebration. 'I can explain later.'

'Please.' Kaliq beckoned him over. 'I would prefer to know so that I may enjoy my dessert.'

Tamara was barely listening, chatting away with Hana who had asked if she might examine the sapphires in closer detail. She supposed she ought to have been annoyed that Kaliq had invited his aide to discuss royal business at their wedding breakfast but she was schooling herself that moments like the one they had shared during the intimate ceremony outweighed times like these.

Jalaal, a man of few words, nodded and began to speak slowly. 'I just ran into the team looking at the instructions for your coronation. They told me that the first step was to check the ancient edict on inheritance for amendments. It was something no one even considered doing before, since the law has always been set in stone, but as the document instructed that it should be followed to the letter, they did—' he looked guilty, as if he had failed in *his* duty '—and it seems that your father made an alteration just days before he died.'

Tamara's ears pricked up. She remembered reading that, unlike many modern countries, the sole ruler of Qwasir still had the right to amend laws single-handedly, and to make new ones. The latter was a common occurrence as advancement demanded, the former was considered something of a taboo, since it presupposed the current king knew better than the rulers of the past.

Kaliq drew in a deep breath. 'Go on.'

Jalaal removed a piece of parchment from the envelope, and nervously began to read the words of Rashid.

'Contrary to centuries of edict, I have seen with my own eyes that my son, a bachelor, will better rule Qwasir by taking a wife at a time of his choosing, rather than being forced to do so at the time of my passing. Henceforth, I rule that marital status is no longer to be a factor in the law of inheritance. This kingdom shall pass from one generation to the next without restriction.'

'It is stamped with the royal seal.' Jalaal stopped abruptly, clearly more given to speaking others' words than his own, then began again awkwardly. 'Of course, it matters little now. I only thought that it might alter the statement you choose to make to Your people, Your Highness. For whilst the kingdom will be overjoyed at your marriage, it is right that they should know what King Rashid wished, that you have lawfully been the King since the moment he died.'

Tamara stared at Jalaal in disbelief, her mouth suddenly dry. Kaliq had never needed to marry in order to inherit after all.

The one reason they were both here now had ceased to exist. The same reason that had once prompted him to propose in the desert, to orchestrate the royal gala, suggest the fake engagement, the one valid reason she had for offering herself to him as his wife. His words tore every second they'd ever spent together into a thousand tiny pieces and blew them all away.

It ought not to have mattered. This wasn't *Jane Eyre*—he didn't have some mad wife locked in the palace attic, a legal impediment why they *couldn't* be married. But that just proved how fragile this whole thing was without love. It *did* matter, because without love to bind them together now, what grounds did she have for being in his life whatsoever?

For the second time in as many weeks the tentative link that held them together had snapped, and this time it took her heart with it for good.

She caught him watching her as she felt the colour drain from her face.

'Thank you, Jalaal, Hana. It is important that I discuss with my wife the nature of what we wish to announce.'

Utter professionalism, of course. From him and from his staff. Whilst she struggled not to dissolve into tears and sink helplessly to the floor, not even Hana looked longingly at the cake they would never eat. The champagne they would never finish. And why would they? In their eyes the marriage had always been planned; the law had simply meant the ceremony happened a little earlier than it otherwise might have done. But that was the Tamara and Kaliq the world saw, not the two people left in the room as he closed the door.

He turned around, looking at her from beneath hooded lids. What was that—pity? She might not be able to bear this coming to an end but the thought that he might be trying to find a way to let her down gently was even worse. It took all the strength she had left to stand up, but if there was a chance of leaving with her dignity intact she had to take it. What else did she have left to cling to?

'There are only a handful of people who know that this ever took place, Kaliq,' she whispered wretchedly, leaning on the table for support. 'This is like that saying: if a tree falls in a wood with no one there to hear it, does it still make a sound?'

He looked perplexed.

'The wedding that almost nobody saw—who needs to know it even happened? Philosophically speaking, I'm not sure it even exists.' Sarcasm entered her tone as it occurred to her just how easy this would be for him to undo.

'It happened,' he ground out.

'But if we had known, I would never have said what I did and you would never have agreed, we both know that.'

He looked horrified. Why? she wondered. Because he wished he had known minutes earlier?

'The papers are already signed.'

'Under a false pretence, with no consummation. That's grounds for annulment. Wouldn't you say?'

For a moment Kaliq considered discounting one of those reasons by taking her there and then, but he knew it would only add to his shame. He shook his head, forced to admit for the first time in his life that he should have thought twice about doing his goddammed duty. He should have thought about feelings—hers.

'You want an annulment?' he said bleakly.

Tears trembled at her eyes, threatening to fall. 'It's either that or stay married to a woman you don't need, Kaliq. What would be the point of that?'

Please, she prayed. *The point is I love you—just tell me to stay regardless.*

She waited for him to answer. Willed him to give a list of unromantic reasons as long as her arm. Prayed for one reason—any reason.

He shook his head. 'I should never have asked this of you, Tamara.'

'You didn't,' she whispered brokenly.

CHAPTER FIFTEEN

THE ten days since her wedding had been the hardest of Tamara's life. They were the days most couples spent on honeymoon, but which she'd spent alone, picking up the remnants of her old life in London.

On the plane home—the charter flight she had insisted upon after the royal Jeep he had demanded she use—Tamara had told herself that, however long it took for her heart to heal, this time had to be easier because, unlike seven years before, there would be no more wondering about what might have been. But it only made it harder. Back then she had only *suspected* she belonged with him. Now she was more sure of that than she had ever been of anything else in her life.

Which was why, as she dressed for the afternoon's shoot, she knew that however much she felt the urge to leave modelling and take up something new, it was pointless. She would wake each morning just as numb whether she was going to work in an ice cream parlour or the Jezebel studio. At least remaining here meant she was still earning enough to give regular donations to the Foundation. In fact, Henry had even upped her salary, and when she had apologised for being away for longer than she'd anticipated he had shushed her. 'Nonsense, sweet-cheeks, take another month off if you're going to be with *him*. Sales are positively booming since the Jezebel girl got herself engaged to a sheikh.'

She hadn't told him, of course. That they were married, that it was over. She hadn't told anyone—not Lisa, or Mike. Even her parents who, since her conversation with Rashid, she'd been tempted to get in touch with. Instead, she had been avoiding calls and evading the, 'Have you set a date?' questions from Emma and the other girls at work. In the evenings she busied herself with as much paperwork for the charity as possible—anything that didn't require discussion. In any other circumstance she would have felt triumphant, because contrary to Kaliq's beliefs, no one seemed to be batting an eyelid that despite being engaged to a desert prince in the eyes of the world, she was continuing with her career. Would have, if just remembering sitting in the car with him that night in Montéz didn't make her heart ache with regret, make her want to sink down with her back against the wall and hold her head in her hands.

Tamara listened to the summer rain beating on the window-pane of her dressing room and twisted the betrothal ring around her finger; she couldn't bring herself to take it off. Her excuse was that if she had, people would be asking a very different set of questions. Because Kaliq had made no announcement about their relationship either. Oh, yes, there had been a press release on the night of their wedding, but it had stated only the details of the change to the law, had given the date of his intended coronation.

There had been nothing about Qwasir in the news since, but she was sure there would have to be soon. The coronation was now only a few days away, and she felt certain that he wouldn't risk having the event overshadowed by press specu-lation about her absence. Though she knew it would be incredibly painful, she was now at the point of wishing she could just get it over with. Just as she longed to be able to stop listening out for the sinister thud of annulment papers to drop through her letterbox. Perhaps the legal go-ahead was what he was waiting for before he announced their break-up to the world—these things took time, didn't they? It had with her parents. But then that had been a proper marriage to start with—and theirs? He had obviously sworn Jalaal, Hana and the celebrant to secrecy and that was to be the end of it. She looked down at her hands, thinking how convenient it was for him that wedding rings were not the custom in Qwasir, before heading out to the room full of countless cameras once more.

'Smile as if your prince has just proposed, Tamara—yes, that's it.'

Unobserved in the shadows, Kaliq leaned back against the door frame and drew in a ragged breath. Was it possible that he wanted her more now than he ever had? That she had got more beautiful? Or was it just that now he no longer had to imagine what it would be like to have her in his bed—he knew. Not so long ago he had believed that was all he wanted. Now he understood that was simply not the way it worked when it came to Tamara Weston.

Clenching his teeth, he wondered how it was that his feelings had changed in such a short space of time, for the scene was, after all, exactly as he remembered. Except today the oversized perfume bottle bore the logo *Natural Jezebel*, and Tamara was dressed in a floaty lemon dress, which was surprisingly modest, her make up minimal and the backdrop all summer meadows and lakes.

The familiar thud of desire went without saying, the yearning to scoop her up and take her away so that no one might look at her but him. But now he knew that the face she wore before the camera wasn't the real her. Not for the back page of some magazine was Tamara playing tennis in the sunshine. Not for Henry the press of her body on horseback. Not for anyone but him the way she had smiled as she'd walked towards him on their wedding day.

The wedding which had run through his mind non-stop for ten long days like the old reel-to-reel he and Leon used to play with. Ten days in which, so unlike the fortnight before, he allowed himself to do little else *but* think. About how deeply he had misjudged her. How much he had wronged her. Most of all, why the hell he hadn't thought to check whether there had been any amendments to the damned law himself. But, the more he thought about it, the more he kept coming back to the same answer.

He had wanted a reason to marry her.

Why? That question had resurrected the one she had asked of him. What *was* the point in staying married to a woman you didn't need? And the more he thought about *that*, the more he understood why his father had made such an unprecedented change.

Kaliq had always believed that the law of inheritance had been designed so that the king might set a good example to his people and produce legitimate sons and, if the law had stood, he would no doubt have carried on believing that. Now he saw that was only a very small part of it. Since Tamara had been gone, even though she had been in his life for a relatively short period of time, each day he had found himself wanting to ask her opinion on various matters when his advisors simply weren't the right people to consult. At night, he had wanted to go to his bed and gather her into his arms. Her absence opened up a gaping hole he could no longer sidestep.

No, there was no point in being married to a woman he no longer needed, but he *did* need Tamara. Not in order to be king, but as a man. He had supposed that was a weakness, a loss of control that would lay him open to the kind of pain his father had suffered after the death of his mother. Only now did he see that facing that need was a mark of true strength.

Yet it changed nothing unless she needed him too, and surely if she did she would never have suggested the annulment? Kaliq ran the thin brown envelope between his fingers. Perhaps he should have couriered it here straight away, he owed her that much. But he couldn't stop remembering the look on her face when the celebrant had pronounced them husband and wife. Was she really *that* good at playing a part? There was only one way to be sure.

Tamara's face ached. It had been an exhausting day after another sleepless night and she wanted to make a run for her umbrella and head home. Or at least back to the flat she called home, where she could bury herself in some mindless task which didn't involve plastering on the blithe expression that the ad for this new fragrance demanded.

'Can someone just grab me a glass of water, please?' She looked past the row of cameras, hoping to pick out Emma.

The minute she did she wished she'd asked for something stronger.

Kaliq. Head and shoulders set autocratically above the rest. Here, in person. She felt herself start to shake.

A flash went off.

'Uh…on second thoughts, do you mind if we take a break?'

'No problem. That last shot's perfect—we're done for the day.'

That last shot; the one where she'd allowed her own

emotions to creep in. The thought of that on every billboard from here to Tokyo made her shudder. The one in which she'd been wondering why he was here, hoping against hope, except this time there was really only one reason—like the Grim Reaper arriving on someone's doorstep in a horror movie.

He walked towards her, a seemingly innocuous envelope in his hand, reminding her of the one Jalaal had carried into the palace drawing room on the best and the worst day of her life. He looked as devastating as ever, but almost as if he'd let go of something. She didn't know what.

'I liked it better,' he said softly, nodding towards where they had been shooting.

'You don't have to say that.'

He looked uncharacteristically offended. 'Things change.'

But people remain the same—wasn't that what he had once argued?

'Perhaps.'

She studied him, ignoring the heads that turned to watch them as she passed by with the king of a desert kingdom by her side, her denim jacket slung over the summer dress. Utterly incongruous.

Somehow they ended up walking to her dressing room; it seemed the only place to escape the eyes upon them. She was thankful he made no comment that it was no guarantee that they wouldn't be disturbed, nor on the larger 'private' sign she had hung on the door since his last visit, though it made her blush as he followed her in.

'How have you been?'

'Working,' she said evasively.

He didn't answer her, just placed down the envelope—the one that contained the end of the sham of a marriage they had entered into—and sank down into a chair. She wished he hadn't. It reminded her of the moment she had found him there just over a month ago, sitting on it as if it were a throne, of how he had dropped his lips to her hand. It also meant he had no intention of doing this quickly, which surely would have been the best way, like ripping off a plaster. Except he wasn't the one with the wound, and hers felt too deep for a short sharp pain to be the end of it.

Tamara pulled a chair from under the dressing table and sat down too, hoping it made her look less awkward than she felt, knotting her hands in her lap, not knowing what to do with them.

She was still wearing the betrothal ring, he noticed. Once he would have seen it as a sign of tasteless greed; today he knew she probably hadn't wanted to cause speculation for the sake of his country. Right now he chose to take it as a symbol of hope.

'I've been thinking about what you said.'

'So I see.' She nodded towards the papers. *Better to get this over with.* 'May I take a look?'

He pushed the envelope towards her and she quickly pulled out the sheaf of papers. As she did, something fell onto the floor.

A photograph. Their wedding photograph.

The one Jalaal had taken but she had never seen, which was to have been released when their marriage was announced to the world. It was startling. Seeing it—the evidence that it hadn't been a dream. But not as startling as the expression it captured. She had never seen a photo of herself looking anything like it—not in her old tennis club photos, not on her travel snaps from Europe, Sydney, or even abroad with the Foundation, and certainly not in any of the Jezebel shots. The only expression she could think of that came remotely close was on the face of another bride wearing the A'zam jewels many years before. It was the look of utter contentment.

'Are you okay?'

Tamara bit her lip and nodded, tucking the photo back in the envelope.

'The negatives are in there as well, if you wish to destroy all the proof.'

'Why are you giving them to me?' she asked, bewildered. They had the potential to cause the biggest scandal in the A'zam family's history, so why hadn't *he* destroyed them?

'I thought you wanted to be sure no one would ever know our marriage happened.'

'You trust *me* with them?'

Kaliq drew in a deep breath, knowing she still believed he thought so little of her. 'I should never have doubted that you were anything *but* trustworthy, Tamara. But it was easier to believe the opposite. Until I began to realise the truth.' He looked uncomfortable. 'Until I found out about the Start-A-School Foundation.'

Tamara felt as if her last defence had just been stripped away. She opened her mouth to deny it, but then shut it again.

'Why didn't you tell me? Why did you let me criticise you again and again, that night at the gala…?'

'It wasn't something I wanted the world to know.'

'I wouldn't have told anyone if you hadn't wished me to.' He looked offended, but not as profoundly as he did the minute she replied.

'I didn't want *you* to know.'

'Why?'

'Because it was easier that way.'

Kaliq had never met anyone like her. He had once accused her of caring too much about what the world thought of her. But she cared so little that she let people make the wrong assumptions, whilst underneath she had this incredible heart. Was it really possible that a woman with such a capacity to love could enter a marriage for purely selfless reasons, fully prepared never to open that heart?

He looked at her, long and hard. 'In the same way that it will be easier if we had our marriage annulled before word leaks out?'

'Ye-yes.'

The look he was giving her did things to her insides. As if he was daring her to say no, to admit she wanted him as much as every other living breathing female on the planet. She didn't. She wanted him more.

'You'd better read it, then,' he countered, tapping the papers.

Tamara stared at the legal jargon, wondering whether signing a document to say she wished to reverse their marriage when she secretly wished the opposite was equivalent to lying in court. She told herself not to be so stupid.

The words swam before her eyes.

Tamara Weston…entered into this marriage under a misapprehension…

'It is necessary, given your position, that it does not state that *you* were misinformed?' she asked, not looking up.

'No.'

She frowned, raising her head. 'Then why doesn't it say that we were both ignorant of the information that made us choose to be married? You had no reason to suspect your father had changed the law a few days before he died.'

An expression that looked like trepidation mixed with remorse suddenly came over his face. 'That's not strictly true.'

'What?' Tamara's heart felt as if it were pulsing in her eardrums. Thoughts were darting across her mind, connecting, disconnecting, trying to absorb what that meant.

He took a deep breath. 'The day we announced our engagement my father asked to see me, not long after he had spoken
with you. He told me that he was beginning to think that particular law could do more harm than good, that it wasn't fair
for you to believe I was only marrying you in order to inherit
the kingdom. At the time I took it as nothing but my father's
errant ramblings—irrelevant, given that at the time we were
only *pretending* to be engaged—and dismissed the idea.'

'And when I offered myself as your wife for real, you
didn't think you ought to make sure?' she questioned, forbid-
ding her heart to swell, wondering how on earth this was
possible, why he hadn't checked for the sake of Qwasir, if
nothing else.

He looked mortified. 'I believe it was because...I was
happy to have a reason to marry you.'

She shook her head, memories flooding her mind, not
wanting to ask the question, but knowing she had to.

'Why?'

He lifted his eyes and caught hers. For him to list the practical reasons why, as if this were some complicated treaty,
would have been easy—he could think of even more in this
moment than he had been able to seven years before—but now
he understood those reasons had never been the ones that
mattered. The moment he had seen the heartbreak on her face
as she had looked at that photograph, he had known. Had
known it was time he admitted the whole truth to her; the one
he had only just begun to admit to himself. It had nothing to
do with duty or even his libido. It was what he felt in his heart,
what he hoped she felt in hers. And though it might have been
the conventional answer for anyone else in the world who had
been asked that question, those three little words could not
have been any more exceptional to him.

'Because I love you, Tamara.' He looked defeated, as if the words weren't enough. 'I didn't know it at first, and then, when I began to suspect—it seemed easier…less of a risk to use duty as an excuse.'

Tamara closed her eyes. She had played out a similar scene so many times in her head—the dream where he asked her to marry him in the desert and when she asked why, that was the answer he gave. They had been too young then, she had had too many ideas and he only one. But now?

'I may have also been economical with the truth.' She dipped her head.

Once a look of accusation would have crossed his face, now she saw only concern furrow his brows.

'I did not ask you to marry me because your country needed you to take a wife in order to inherit the kingdom. That simply gave me the courage to ask. The reason I asked was because I spent seven years trying to convince myself that saying no to you was the right decision because you had asked me for all the wrong reasons. But, whatever I did, I never succeeded. In Montéz, when I discovered what it was to be with you, really with you, I knew I would rather spend my life with you for a bunch of wrong reasons rather than not at all.'

He stared at her in disbelief, the corners of his mouth curving in tenderness. 'In that case, Tamara, I wish you to remove the betrothal ring.'

'What?' she whispered.

'Because it would be the greatest honour if you would wear this.' He reached into his pocket and produced a thoroughly modern box. In it was a brand new, plain gold band.

She looked up at him, her eyes wide and brimming with tears of joy, not knowing what to say. *He* was saying that he didn't want this marriage to end—that, by the looks of it, he wanted the world to know.

'But wedding bands aren't…aren't customary in Qwasir,' she said breathlessly, stumbling over her words.

'But you are British, and I am a modern man—' he frowned as if it was obvious '—and our marriage is to be one of equality. Besides, how else will people know that you are my wife when you are working?'

'Working?'

'I was wrong to make the assumptions and the demands that I did. Our lives are joining together; I do not want you to cease to be the person that you were before.'

Tamara couldn't believe her ears. 'Oh, Kaliq, I don't want to carry on modelling. But I do want to work, yes. Let me help with the new school in Lan, build others just the same.'

He nodded thoughtfully as he took her hand and slipped the ring onto her finger. 'Whatever you choose.'

'What are we going to tell the people of Qwasir?' she whispered in delight.

'You mean you want to call the paparazzi?' he teased. 'How would you feel if I released the photo today, and neglected to mention that the wedding occurred two weeks ago?'

'I think it would demand a very long anniversary celebration in future, so as not to raise suspicion,' she said, grinning.

'You mean rather like the very long honeymoon we are going to take the second the coronation is out of the way?'

Tamara couldn't sit down any longer. In one forward motion she was in his arms, knocking the papers to the floor.

But, just as she was about to kiss him, he stopped her.

'Did you notice that I ignored your suggestion to cite lack of consummation as a reason for annulment?'

She tucked a strand of hair affectionately behind his ear,

looking puzzled, but nodded. 'I'm glad. That was no one's business but ours.'

Kaliq laughed. 'You are more conventional than you realise.'

'What do you mean?'

'I left it off because, regardless of the damned annulment, I came here with the objective of making you my wife in every sense of the word.'

Tamara felt a bubble of excitement rise in her throat as he released the clip from her hair.

'Well, I wouldn't want to subvert something as precious as the King's *objectives*.'

He looked down at her, his face utterly serious. 'Nothing is more precious to me than you, my wife.'

'Even Qwasir's most valuable sapphires?' She grinned.

'Especially those,' he replied forcefully and, with that, his mouth swooped down to capture hers.

And, as they kissed each other urgently, the London rain pouring down outside her dressing room window, Kaliq and Tamara finally found one another. The model and the sheikh. The King and Queen of Qwasir.

But, most of all, two people who dared to love.

Turn the page for an exclusive extract
from Harlequin Presents®
THE PRINCE'S CAPTIVE WIFE
by
Marion Lennox

Bedded and wedded—by blackmail!

Nine years ago Prince Andreas Karedes left Australia
to inherit his royal duties, but unbeknownst to him he
left a woman pregnant.

Innocent young Holly tragically lost their baby and
remained on her parents' farm to be near her tiny son's
final resting place, wishing Andreas would return!

A royal scandal is about to break: a dirt-digging journalist has discovered Holly's secret, so Andreas forces
his childhood sweetheart to come and face him! Passion
runs high as Andreas issues an ultimatum: to avoid
scandal, Holly must become his royal bride!

"SHE WAS ONLY SEVENTEEN?"

"We're talking ten years ago. I was barely out of my teens myself."

"Does that make a difference?" The uncrowned king of Aristo stared across his massive desk at his younger brother, his aquiline face dark with fury. "Have we not had enough scandal?"

"Not of my making." Prince Andreas Christos Karedes, third in line to the Crown of Aristo, stood his ground against his older brother with the disdain he always used in this family of testosterone-driven males. His father and brothers might be acknowledged womanizers, but Andreas made sure his affairs were discreet.

"Until now," Sebastian said. "Not counting your singularly spectacular divorce, which had a massive impact. But this is worse. You will have to sort it before it explodes over all of us."

"How the hell can I sort it?"

"Get rid of her."

"You're not saying…"

"Kill her?" Sebastian smiled up at his younger brother, obviously rejecting the idea—though a tinge of regret in his voice said the option wasn't altogether unattractive.

And Andreas even sympathized. Since their father's death, all three brothers had been dragged through the mire of the media spotlight, and the political unrest was threatening to destroy them. In their thirties, impossibly handsome, wealthy beyond belief, indulged and feted, the brothers were now facing realities they had no idea what to do with.

"Though if I was our father…" Sebastian added, and Andreas shuddered. Who knew what the old king would have done if he'd discovered Holly's secret? Thank God he'd never found out. Not that King Aegeus could have taken the moral high ground. It was, after all, his father's past actions that had gotten them into this mess.

"You'll make a better king than our father ever was," Andreas said softly. "What filthy dealing made him dispose of the royal diamond?"

"That's my concern," Sebastian said. There could be no royal coronation until the diamond was found—they all knew that—but the way the media was baying for blood there might not be a coronation even then. Without the diamond the rules had changed. If any more scandals broke… "This girl…"

"Holly."

"You remember her?"

"Of course I remember her."

"Then she'll be easy to find. We'll buy her off—do whatever it takes, but she mustn't talk to anyone."

"If she wanted to make a scandal she could have done it years ago."

"So it's been simmering in the wings for years. To have it surface now…" Sebastian rose and fixed Andreas with a look that was almost as deadly as the one used by the old king. "It can't happen, brother. We have to make sure she's not in a position to bring us down."

"I'll contact her."

"You'll go nowhere near her until we're sure of her reaction. Not even a phone call, brother. For all we know her phones are already tapped. I'll have her brought here."

"I can arrange…"

"You stay right out of it until she's on our soil. You're heading the corruption inquiry. With Alex on his honeymoon with Maria—of all the times for him to demand to marry, this must surely be the worst—I need you more than ever. If you leave now and this leaks, we can almost guarantee losing the crown."

"So how do you propose to persuade her to come?"

"Oh, I'll persuade her," Sebastian said grimly. "She's only a slip of a girl. She might be your past, but there's no way she's messing with our future."

* * * * *

Be sure to look for
THE PRINCE'S CAPTIVE WIFE
by Marion Lennox,
available September 2009 from Harlequin Presents®!

Copyright © 2009 by Harlequin S.A.

HARLEQUIN *Presents*

TWO CROWNS, TWO ISLANDS, ONE LEGACY

A royal family, torn apart by pride and its lust for power, reunited by purity and passion

Pick up the next adventures in this passionate series!

THE PRINCE'S CAPTIVE WIFE
by Marion Lennox, September 2009

THE SHEIKH'S FORBIDDEN VIRGIN
by Kate Hewitt, October 2009

THE GREEK BILLIONAIRE'S INNOCENT PRINCESS
by Chantelle Shaw, November 2009

THE FUTURE KING'S LOVE-CHILD
by Melanie Milburne, December 2009

RUTHLESS BOSS, ROYAL MISTRESS
by Natalie Anderson, January 2010

THE DESERT KING'S HOUSEKEEPER BRIDE
by Carol Marinelli, February 2010

www.eHarlequin.com

HPI 2851

TAKEN: AT THE BOSS'S COMMAND

His every demand will *be met!*

Whether he's a British billionaire, an Argentinian
polo player, an Italian tycoon or a Greek magnate,
these men demand the very best of everything—
and everyone....

Working with him is one thing—marrying him is *quite*
another. But when the boss chooses his bride,
there's no option but to say I do!

**Catch all the heart-racing stories,
available September 2009:**

The Boss's Inexperienced Secretary #69
by HELEN BROOKS

Argentinian Playboy, Unexpected Love-Child #70
by CHANTELLE SHAW

The Tuscan Tycoon's Pregnant Housekeeper #71
by CHRISTINA HOLLIS

Kept by Her Greek Boss #72
by KATHRYN ROSS

www.eHarlequin.com

HPE0909

HARLEQUIN *Presents*

International Billionaires

Life is a game of power and pleasure.
And these men play to win!

THE VIRGIN SECRETARY'S IMPOSSIBLE BOSS
by *Carole Mortimer*

Billionaire Linus loves a challenge.
During one snowbound Scottish night
the temperature rises with his sensible
personal assistant. With sparks flying,
how can Andi resist?

Book #2854

Available September 2009

HPI 2854

www.eHarlequin.com

When a wealthy man takes a wife,
it's not always for love...

Meet three wealthy Sydney businessmen who've been
the best of friends for ages. None of them believe in
marrying for love. But all this is set to change....

This exciting new trilogy by

Miranda Lee

begins September 2009 with

THE BILLIONAIRE'S BRIDE OF VENGEANCE

Book #2852

Pick up the next installments of this fabulous trilogy:

THE BILLIONAIRE'S BRIDE OF CONVENIENCE
October 2009

THE BILLIONAIRE'S BRIDE OF INNOCENCE
November 2009

www.eHarlequin.com

HP1 2852

REQUEST YOUR FREE BOOKS!

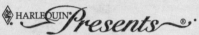

2 FREE NOVELS
PLUS 2
FREE GIFTS!

YES! Please send me 2 FREE Harlequin Presents® novels and my 2 FREE gifts (gifts are worth about $10). After receiving them, if I don't wish to receive any more books, I can return the shipping statement marked "cancel". If I don't cancel, I will receive 6 brand-new novels every month and be billed just $4.05 per book in the U.S. or $4.74 per book in Canada. That's a savings of close to 15% off the cover price! It's quite a bargain! Shipping and handling is just 50¢ per book*. I understand that accepting the 2 free books and gifts places me under no obligation to buy anything. I can always return a shipment and cancel at any time. Even if I never buy another book, the two free books and gifts are mine to keep forever.

106 HDN EYRQ   306 HDN EYR2

Name	(PLEASE PRINT)	
Address		Apt. #
City	State/Prov.	Zip/Postal Code

Signature (if under 18, a parent or guardian must sign)

Mail to the **Harlequin Reader Service:**
IN U.S.A.: P.O. Box 1867, Buffalo, NY 14240-1867
IN CANADA: P.O. Box 609, Fort Erie, Ontario L2A 5X3

Not valid to current subscribers of Harlequin Presents books.

**Are you a current subscriber of Harlequin Presents books and want to
receive the larger-print edition? Call 1-800-873-8635 today!**

* Terms and prices subject to change without notice. Prices do not include applicable taxes. Sales tax applicable in N.Y. Canadian residents will be charged applicable provincial taxes and GST. Offer not valid in Quebec. This offer is limited to one order per household. All orders subject to approval. Credit or debit balances in a customer's account(s) may be offset by any other outstanding balance owed by or to the customer. Please allow 4 to 6 weeks for delivery. Offer available while quantities last.

Your Privacy: Harlequin Books is committed to protecting your privacy. Our Privacy Policy is available online at www.eHarlequin.com or upon request from the Reader Service. From time to time we make our lists of customers available to reputable third parties who may have a product or service of interest to you. If you would prefer we not share your name and address, please check here. ☐

HP09R

You're invited to join our Tell Harlequin Reader Panel!

By joining our new reader panel you will:

- Receive Harlequin® books—they are FREE and yours to keep with no obligation to purchase anything!
- Participate in fun online surveys
- Exchange opinions and ideas with women just like you
- Have a say in our new book ideas and help us publish the best in women's fiction

In addition, you will have a chance to win great prizes and receive special gifts! See Web site for details. Some conditions apply. Space is limited.

To join, visit us at
www.TellHarlequin.com.

I ♥ HARLEQUIN® *Presents*

BROUGHT TO YOU BY FANS OF
HARLEQUIN PRESENTS.

We are its editors and authors
and biggest fans—and we'd
love to hear from YOU!

Subscribe today to our online blog at
www.iheartpresents.com

HPBLOG